The Aspiring Writers
2013
Winners Anthology

The Short Stories

The Poems:

Illustration credits (used with permission of the artists, who retain all rights to their works):

Liam R.E. Quin
photo of stack of antique books

Betsy Riley www.BetsyRiley.com
photos, collages, and illustrations

ISBN-13: 978--1-62220-017-7 Blue Dragon Press

BlueDragonPress.com

cover image by Liam R.E. Quin

Foreword

Ronnie Dauber, *organizer of the 2013 Competitions*

The idea for this anthology originated online in a LinkedIn group created to encourage and inspire both new and experienced authors.

In a subgroup, called *Aspiring Writers Short Story Competitions and Discussions*, members participate in discussions and writing competitions to help polish their writing skills.

Each month, the moderator announces a challenge. Writers have two weeks to craft a story no longer than 715 words addressing the challenge. The story must conform to a specific genre and theme, and feature a highlight (often an object), all announced as part of the challenge.

The reward for the winners of these monthly competitions is to have their stories published in a yearly anthology, with proceeds donated to a charity. This volume (2013 Winners) also includes the winners of the 2013 monthly poetry competition. This book is the third in the ongoing series--collections that display the talents of aspiring writers from around the globe.

JANUARY 2013 Short Story Winners

genre: **fiction-suspense/thriller**
theme: **New Year's Eve**
highlight: **a hairbrush**

FIRST PLACE
"Golden Curl Girl"
by Alli Vaughan

SECOND PLACE
"A Desolate End by Hairbrush"
by Daron Henson
Author site: **newkidintown1995.blogspot.com**

THIRD PLACE
"Brushed Away"
by Dan Marvin
Author site: **DanMarvin.wordpress.com**

 **Alli Vaughan** is a marketing director living in Portland, Oregon. In her free time she enjoys painting, creative writing, and jogging. Her favorite genre of books is fantasy, but she also loves a good science fiction story as well. Her writing tends to involve the mystical and the paranormal.

First Place

Golden Curl Girl
by Alli Vaughan

New Year's Eve is a tough night to find a body in your car.

God! Who'd I given my keys to that night? My mind struggles with questions, as two shaking hands that don't feel like mine slam the trunk shut. My eyes dart about the ice-fleeced parking lot, but I seem alone.

I didn't need to open the trunk again to know that a tuft of blonde hair was wedged inside. The shock left me stone sober; this wasn't a product of my imagination, nor an effect from the three shots I'd downed before leaving the party. This was really happening.

"My god," I whisper to myself, my breath freezing in the cold-prickled air. And I had

5

thought cops prowling the streets for drunks were the only thing I'd have to worry about tonight.

Just my luck. I'd gotten clean recently, and was scraping a living by pawning estate sale scores to premiere buyers for cash. It hadn't been easy. And with three warrants and a streak of bad luck a mile wide, I'd almost expected to be pulled over tonight. But not like this, not for a murder I didn't commit. Time frozen, I go numb.

What the heck am I going to do?

The whirl of a siren racing by snaps me to the present. My hand shakes; I've got to get out of here.

My car putters onto the frozen street. Cars blur past me, all seeming to travel faster than my eyes can follow. I narrowly miss a white van as my car skates into the right lane. My heart racing, I travel out of the city, onto the emptiest highway I can find.

It's only a few minutes before I notice the car tailing me.

I tried to shake it, but they weren't letting up. Welded to my bumper, they loomed behind me.

The driver isn't trying to hide the tail, but I don't see police lights. Someone else then. Did they know about the body? That was the only explanation.

My speed breaks 70, 80, 95! I've no clue how fast I'm going when I pull off the freeway. My tires spin clumps of earth in the air as my wheels slice into the dirt road, trying to elude the other car. He's still on me. Gotta try something else, something risky.

My insides roll, but somehow I make the curve. My eyes dart back, praying my pursuers are gone. Still there. Another tight corner should throw them. I almost heave the contents of my stomach this time -- acid and whiskey. Something flies from the back seat, landing in my lap.

A hairbrush? Golden curls spread out from the teeth in all directions, like tinsel on a tree. I toss it in the back, but something familiar about the brush gnaws at me.

The other car's so close I can almost smell the exhaust fumes. I'm done running, my nerves twist. I skid off the road and let fate catch me. My fingers slip onto the gun I pull from under my seat as comfortably as warm socks.

The car stops behind me and the high beams light the figure approaching, as I step out of the car. I squeeze the hilt of the gun hidden in my jacket, but don't draw. Yet.

I stare. "Tony," I said, my mouth dropping as the squinty eyes of one of my buyers sharpen into view.

"Jesus, Johnny! What're you doing?"

Did Tony know about the body? My mind races. "Why are you tailing me?" The words choke out my throat.

"You've lost it tonight, haven't you?" he asked, shaking his head. "How much did you drink?" I stared dumbly back.

He sighs. "You were going to sell me the mannequin you called me about, but took off suddenly. I followed you from the party. My cash's already in your pocket and I want her!"

"The b...bbbrush," I stutter, realization clearing the mental fog. The brush and other garbage had been wrapped around the prize, the vintage mannequin I'd scored from the foreclosure salvage this week.

No bother trying to save face. I open my trunk and deliver the golden haired prize as promised. I stand around hours after Tony leaves, sobering up enough to drive home. I'm done with parties, even on New Years.

Under the Influence, collage by Betsy Riley

Daron Henson is an aspiring writer working on his first book. He studied at the University of California at Santa Barbara, where he minored in philosophy. This course of study inspired his writing.

You can find much of his work at **newkidintown1995.blogspot.com**

Second Place

A Desolate End by Hairbrush
by Daron Henson

Walking through the suburbs on this New Year's Eve, there were no celebrations to be had for Joseph. Single, and without any close family, he spent the occasion alone.

As he walked, he felt the freedom unexpected for a man in his situation. He looked up into the sky and began to sing a song which had recently caught his attention.

"Merriments are over, for this is the end. Your time on Earth is finished, once you find what is around the bend."

With no knowledge of the band who sang it, it appealed to his optimistic sense of morbidity.

As he walked through the neighborhood, completely untouched by his position of

11

solitude, he took the long way home to savor his journey.

As he walked, a homeless man appeared from out of the darkness; an event extremely out of place in this city of relative luxury. To compound the perplexity, he noticed the man brushing his long locks of blonde hair with what appeared to be a dog's hairbrush.

The obscurity turned into irrelevance until the homeless man asked Joseph, "Toppins for the poor, for I need a new hairbrush."

Joseph looked at the man, dug into his pocket, pulled out pocket change, and went on his way.

He continued his journey through the small suburban town until he made his way back to his apartment. As he walked he began to sing.

"Without remorse, it comes your time to go. Without a word, it reaches a bitter close."

He got back to his apartment, unlocked the door, and went in. It was late, but there would be a few more hours before it was time to usher in the New Year. He planned to stay awake for the festivities; where all he could do was watch.

It was 9:00 p.m. and he would spend the last hours of the New Year as it had begun, alone.

A few minutes after he got back to his apartment, he heard rustling around the door. Without the thought of caution, he opened the door to see who it might be. No one was there. He didn't see any reason to be preoccupied with the thought. He went out the door, looking around to see who it might be. Still, nobody was apparent. He looked deep into the night to see who he might see. A shadowy figure loomed far off into the darkness. He noticed, on the ground, what appeared to be a dog's hairbrush accompanied by long locks of blond hair.

He closed the door and thought nothing of it. He left the hairbrush where it lay.

As he turned on the television, he viewed the merriment the world was enjoying. He made himself a ham and cheese sandwich. As he enjoyed the sandwich complete with lettuce and tomato, the song that had been rolling around his mind earlier came on the television and he sat to enjoy it as he ate.

"The working, the playing will all be gone. Nothing left but slumber for all."

Trivial as it was, the song had been prominent in his thoughts for weeks.

He finished his sandwich; excellent with the tomatoes. He even put avocado slices on it and garnished it with gourmet potato chips.

He heard rustling near the door again. He opened the door, but it was over. To no avail, the same homeless man that he had seen brushing his long, blonde hair with what appeared to be a dog's brush hit him once with the hairbrush with such velocity that Joseph fell to the ground. He kept hitting him with that same brush until, it truly was, over.

The next morning, the police arrived. Bludgeoned to death, Joseph's body lay on the ground next to what appeared to be a dog's hairbrush. The police searched his apartment to find only one anomaly. There appeared to be no other hairbrush to be found in Joseph's apartment.

Late the next night, the homeless man sat in a park brushing his long, blonde hair.

Brush with Fate, collage by Betsy Riley

Dan Marvin writes from his South Florida estate. His stories have appeared in many online publications including *eFiction*, *Short Humor*, *AlienSkin*, *Golden Visions*, and many more. He also has written **Briefs for The Reading Room** (an anthology of one-page stories) and a sequel called **Change of Briefs**.

For more about Dan's writing, visit **DanMarvin.wordpress.com**

Third Place

Brushed Away
by Dan Marvin

Lilly remembered her grandmother using this brush during summer trips to her grandparents' farm, but she wasn't sure why she had inherited the brush in the will. The colorful, sparkly jewels on the back of the brush were cut glass and it wasn't worth a great deal of money. Still, she was happy to have the reminder of the happier times of her youth. Things with Barry had been rocky lately and she wasn't looking forward to New Year's Eve with his coworkers.

She looked at her reflection in the mirror and sighed. She had dark circles under her eyes that concealer couldn't conceal and she was feeling every bit of 47 years old. She picked up the brush and started brushing her hair. She liked the heft of it, it was more substantial than the brush she typically used and pulled the tangles from her brunette tresses easily.

After only a few passes with the brush, the mirror began to mist and she could see shadowy forms in it. Lilly let out a little shriek as she looked behind her to see if what she was seeing in the mirror was really there. It wasn't. Turning back, she saw only herself and the bathroom behind her. Willing her breathing to slow, she picked up the brush and started ... there! There it was again. Fascinated now she kept brushing. The forms gained substance, it looked like an old movie on TV. One of the forms was her grandmother, but as a younger woman. The other must be her grandfather, although she had few memories of him since he had died when she was very young. She stopped brushing her hair as a test and, sure enough, the images faded away. Brushing she could see them, but when she stopped they vanished.

Lilly began brushing in earnest. Her grandmother was brushing her hair with this same brush, looking back at her in the mirror as if her own reflection. In the background she could see her mother as a young girl, and could see her grandfather enter the room. There was no sound, but she could see her grandfather smiling, kissing the young girl and then appearing behind his wife who was still brushing her hair just as Lilly was brushing hers. Her grandfather was dressed for a party, somehow she knew it was a New Year's Eve party. Her grandmother was trying to get ready but her grandfather kept kissing his wife on top of her head and messing her hair. She could almost hear her grandmother's convictionless rebukes and when her grandfather left the room, she saw the contented smile on her grandmother's lips. That was it, the show ended and there wasn't even the flapping of the projector to make her think it had been real.

She sat stunned for a moment and looked at the mirror that now just showed her herself. But no, there was a form here too, Barry had entered the bathroom. He looked at her and then away, busying himself with his own preparations for the party. "Barry," she said impulsively. "Come kiss me. I miss your kisses." He looked shocked, but walked over to her and kissed her on top of the head, almost exactly as she had seen her grandfather do in the mirror movie.

He walked out of the bathroom and she smiled a little, the first smile she had worn all day. It wasn't much, but it was a start. She looked at the brush in her hand and slowly placed it in the drawer with her others. She could get through this party, and tomorrow she would see what else the brush had to show her.

The long and the short of it, illustration by Betsy Riley

FEBRUARY 2013 Short Story Winners

genre: **fiction-mystery**
theme: **the past**
highlight: **a picture**

Challenge: *Kenneth Thomas is a 92-year old war veteran sitting in a wheel chair in his private room at a secluded nursing home. He motions for the care worker to hand him the small black and white picture in an elegant gold frame from his nightstand. She asks him what is so special about the picture and why he stares into it for hours each day.* Authors write his response.

FIRST PLACE
"Operation Kenneth Thomas"
by Dan Marvin
Author site: **DanMarvin.wordpress.com**

SECOND PLACE
"Screaming Silence"
by Mario Dimain
Author site: **artisticam.wix.com/mariodimain**

THIRD PLACE
"Cabin on a Stream"
by Laura Rittenhouse
Author site: **www.LauraRittenhouse.com**

 **Dan Marvin** writes from his South Florida estate. His stories have appeared in many online publications including *eFiction*, *Short Humor*, *AlienSkin*, *Golden Visions*, and many more. He also has written ***Briefs for The Reading Room*** (an anthology of one-page stories) and a sequel called ***Change of Briefs***.

For more about Dan's writing, visit
DanMarvin.wordpress.com

First Place

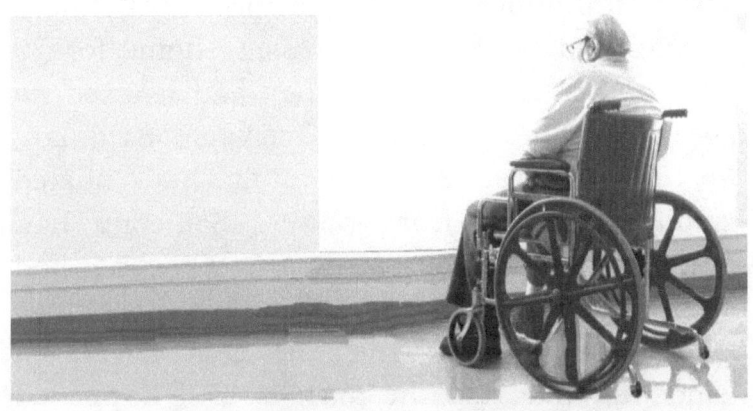

Operation Kenneth Thomas
by Dan Marvin

"Nurse, please hand me that picture." The elderly man waved at his night stand which held a tattered black and white picture in a gold frame.

"What is so special about this picture, Mr. Thomas?" the nurse asked as she handed it to him, as she did every morning about this time. The photo was yellowed with age and instead of a person, the picture showed lights and a desk flanked by chairs. In lieu of answering, he just stared into the picture as he did every morning about this time. With a sigh, the nurse looked at the large mirror on the wall of the room and shrugged slightly.

Behind the mirror, special agent Donnelly looked unhappy but not surprised. Kenneth Thomas had been in this nursing home for 20 years and in all that time they had learned no more about the picture or Operation Stedman, the super-secret offensive that had ousted President Dorain from power. Someone had authorized Operation Stedman, someone had financed it, and someone still pulled the strings behind the scenes while the thin facade of democracy placated the masses. If it happened once, it could happen again, they needed to know who, and this man was the last survivor.

"Red leader, this is Donnelly, come in," the agent spoke into a microphone on his desk. He had never met the contact at the other end of this line, for this mission secrecy was imperative.

"Go ahead Donnelly," a voice quickly responded.

"He's looking at the picture sir, but has given no indication about what it means." Every morning the report was the same. He knew by rote what the reply would be.

"Understood. Report if anything changes. Red leader out."

Kenneth Thomas looked up from the photo with tears in his eyes. "I suppose I should tell you," he said to the nurse. She looked surprised and then motioned urgently into the mirror before approaching the old man. This was a change for sure, Donnelly turned on the recording equipment while the nurse bent over to hear his words more clearly.

"They promised us that if we did our jobs, we would get to go here." He started enigmatically.

"Who did Mr. Thomas? Who promised you?" she asked.

"The Producers of course. They all promised that we would get to sit here. Not in the audience, oh no, but right in this chair here." His gnarled digit pointed to the chair to the left of the desk. "They promised but I never even got to meet her. I risked everything and I never got to meet her."

"You never got to meet who?" The nurse asked, trying not to press too hard while still getting the answer they desperately wanted to know.

"They trained us, showed us how to circumvent the White House security, planned the whole thing, knowing full well that they were never going to give us what we really wanted. I guess that's what stings the most. We pulled it off, we got past the Secret Service, had Dorain dead to rights, and changed the world and she never even said thanks."

"Who never said thanks?" she asked, losing even the pretense of disinterest.

"Oprah! We never got to meet her. She canceled the show and none of us ever got to even meet her. "

Behind the one-way mirror, special agent Donnelly was listening to chaos in his headset. At last they knew who was behind Operation Stedman, but instead of excitement, all he heard was the word "Oprah" repeated over and over with dread.

"Donnelly, this is Red leader. Discontinue all surveillance and destroy recordings. The FBI does not have sufficient resources to take on Oprah. Over and out."

Imphant, photo by Betsy Riley

 **Mario Dimain** is a visual artist who is passionate in expressing his creative thoughts and vision through photography, video and painting. He also loves to merge pictures with written words. His unpublished poem for his grandmother was written when he was ten. Now at 62, he enjoys spending time with his family, mostly with his four grandchildren between photography and creative writing.

In his own words, "Photography inspires me to write. I have written articles and short stories that were triggered by the images in my portfolio. Writing propels me to fly with my imagination and bring out the budding author in me. Writing also gives me inner peace. It makes me understand myself and the power above where the source of my abilities comes from."

Mario's main character in *Screaming Silence* was based on his father who was a combat photographer in the Korean War in the 50's. The little Vietnamese boy in the story was reminiscent of Mario's memory as a child growing up in a village in the Philippines near the American Naval Base.

Author website: **artisticam.wix.com/mariodimain**

Second Place

Screaming Silence
by Mario Dimain

The frail-looking Vietnamese boy in the black and white photo radiates a magnetic smile. His youthful innocence is so engaging. In one hand, he is holding a half-eaten Baby Ruth chocolate bar and in the other, he is holding up the big U.S. Army helmet that appears to be swallowing his head. The little boy's tiny frame suggests he is only six or seven.

"This is Hung," says Kenneth as he presses his aching back against his wheelchair. His wrinkled index finger is pointing to the little boy in the photograph.

Nita, the young Filipina caregiver nods with a smile. "Good looking boy. He must be a very special friend," she says with eagerness to hear more. Her curiosity echoes that of everyone

29

in the Old Oak Nursing Home who has known the 92-year-old war veteran.

Old Ken's grip on the photo frame gets tighter. He pulls in a deep breath to gather his thoughts. His long silence must come to an end. "It has been forty-nine years," he begins.

Under the blistering heat of the mid-afternoon sun, Captain Kenneth Thomas and his team of photojournalists had arrived at the Temporary Shelter for Displaced Children in the remote village of Mung Phai. They were there to produce a documentary film about the many faces of the Vietnam War. The year was 1964.

Stooped on the ground, scanning the vicinity with his camera viewfinder, Kenneth could see the flattened bamboo shacks and fallen trees that were the aftermath of the Viet Cong's attack on the farming village the day before. He was about to take the shot, when out of nowhere, a child's face filled the frame, directly staring curiously at him. The little boy had been watching Kenneth take pictures. The clicking sound of the camera shutter fascinated him.

Kenneth smiled. "What is your name kid? *Bang tenh layi*?"

"Hung!" was the reply. The boy was giggling, amused by Kenneth's American accent.

"I am Kenneth."

"Ken-net?" Hung asked.

Kenneth got excited. He just met the son he never had. "I am pleased to meet you, Hung." He pulled a Baby Ruth from his pocket and offered it to Hung.

"*Kam ung!*" Hung responded happily as he bowed his head in a gesture of deep gratitude. He opened the wrapper and took a bite.

"You are a good kid, Hung," Kenneth said proudly as he rubbed Hung's black hair in a fatherly manner. Then, Kenneth took off his U.S. Army helmet and placed it on Hung's head. He looked at Hung with full approval, stepped back and took the shot of the smiling boy. It was the defining moment of friendship between an orphan boy and a 43-year-old childless man. Their instant bond was frozen in time -- in a black and white photo.

The shooting of the Mung Phai documentary would last a week. In between filming, Kenneth spent his time with Hung. With his limited Vietnamese vocabulary, he managed to communicate with his new little friend. During their choppy conversation, Kenneth talked about a little boy who grew up to be a carpenter. Hung was amazed by the story. He couldn't get enough of it. He wanted to know the name of the boy.

Kenneth carved a small cross out of bamboo, gave it to Hung and said, "The boy's name was Jesus." Hung was in awe.

Before leaving Mung Phai, Kenneth made a promise to Hung that he would return and the two of them would drive back to Saigon. He would then show Hung the U.S. Military Base. Little Hung was hopeful. He patiently waited for his American friend.

Kenneth had a Baby Ruth for Hung when he returned. He was a bit too late. Hung was among the lifeless bodies of children who died when enemies burnt down the Temporary Shelter. Hung was still clutching the bamboo cross when Kenneth found him.

After a long pause, the old veteran's voice is reduced to a whisper, "I was too late." His eyes are welling with tears as he stares at the spectacular sunset across the Pacific Ocean. He smiles at Nita, his caregiver for the past ten years.

It was a beautiful day to put the screaming silence to rest. Holding Hung's photo in his arms, old Ken breathed his last.

Old Film, altered photo by Betsy Riley

Laura Rittenhouse was born in the US, but now calls Australia home. Her career in IT gave her the opportunity to live and work in six different countries on five different continents and, while rewarding, just wasn't how she wanted to spend her days. In 2006 she gave up that career to focus on her passion, writing.

Laura's first novel, ***Starting Over***, was published in 2009 and is available in both electronic and print formats. Two more novels are complete, but, as yet, unpublished. She's also finished a non-fiction travel book, which offers the reader an amusing account of her recent eight-month camping trip in Australia's Outback. In between writing books she occasionally writes short stories in a variety of genres, several of which have been published in a variety of media.

When Laura's not writing, she can be found wandering the 18-acre farm she shares with her chickens, her dog, her cat, over half-a-million honey bees and, of course, her husband.

For more about Laura's writing, visit
www.laurarittenhouse.com

Third Place

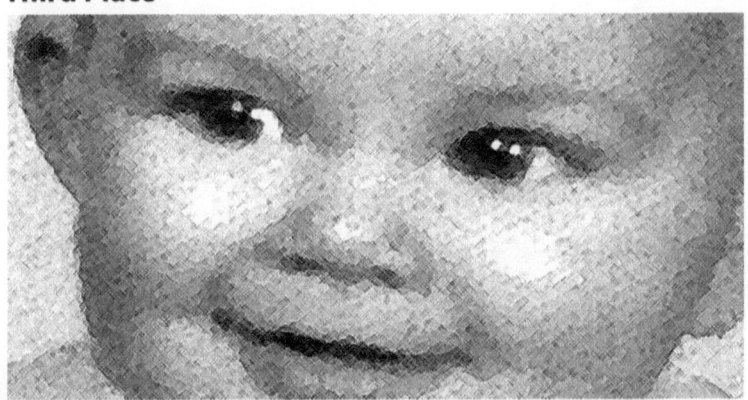

Cabin on a Stream
by Laura Rittenhouse

Kenneth hated the nursing home, but once he bumped into Miranda while visiting a friend, he couldn't relax until he'd moved in. At 92 he probably shouldn't be living alone anyway.

After tapping lightly on his door, Miranda walked in and asked Kenneth if he wanted her to wheel him down to lunch. He waved his hand and answered, "No thanks, I'm not hungry. But can ya pass me that picture on your way out?"

The picture had been the topic of much speculation in the staff lounge because Kenneth spent hours each day staring at it. Miranda finally asked what many of her colleagues had wondered, "Kenneth, what's with this photograph?"

Kenneth closed his eyes. Was there any point in telling her?

"It all goes back to before the war, when I was a little tyke and got thrown by our horse. The doc gave me some potion to cut the pain, but it didn't really help. Ma would sit with me, tellin' me stories until I fell asleep. She built this beautiful dream world for me to play in. A world where we lived in a cabin nestled in a bend of a quiet stream. I imagined that cabin and that stream on so many nights that I could paint it like from a photo once I got a bit older."

Miranda looked at the picture. "This isn't a picture of a painting is it? It looks like a photograph of a real place."

"Nah," Kenneth grabbed the picture, "that's not my painting." His eyes focused on a point well beyond the old black-and-white photo, well beyond the walls of the nursing home.

"Imagine how much fun my wife, June, and I had, dreamin' of movin' to that cabin on the stream. For 2 years, we lived in a tiny apartment with my painting remindin' us where we wanted to be. The fact that it wasn't real didn't bother us none, no siree, dreams were enough. Then that blasted war came, curse the Germans and the Japs both, and I went away to help. It seemed the right thing at the time and June was proud of me for it. She waited for me with that painting and our dreams, back in that little apartment, while I went as far from a dream as anyone could travel."

Kenneth's eyes turned towards the picture in his hand. He polished the gold frame with the cuff of his sleeve then scratched his cheek. "June was a great letter writer, and those letters sure helped keep me sane. Course, they didn't come too regular, it's not like a US Mail truck could just track me down wherever the Army sent me. But they came, and that's what mattered. Only when I got home and found someone else livin' in that little apartment did I realize that the last letter I'd gotten from June had been written months earlier."

He looked straight at Miranda. "She looked a bit like you. Course she was a lot younger than you when I last saw her. Pretty thing, prettier than you, sorry for sayin'."

"That's okay, I'm not all that pretty, maybe 40 years ago, but not now. Anyway, what happened to June? Where was she?"

"That's what I keep wonderin'. I never heard nuthin' from her after that last letter and it didn't hold a clue. Her kin all died before we even met and it was just the two of us, so there was no one I could ask. At first I wanted to run to the police but my landlord took me to his old garage and showed me the boxes of stuff he cleared out of that little apartment after June stopped payin' the rent. Everything was there. Everything except my painting and June's clothes. She'd taken my painting, packed her things and left me.

"Then, 60 years ago, this picture showed up in my mailbox. See that cabin and that stream? That's my dream alright. See that woman holdin' that little girl? You can't see her face 'cause of her hat but you can see that painting of mine leanin' against the front door and you can see that baby smilin' at the camera. That baby with June's eyes. That baby with your eyes."

March 2013 Short Story Winners

genre: **fiction-mystery**
theme: **gathering of Grandpa Michael's family in his home as his will is read**
highlight: **a few drops of blood on the floor by a broken glass cabinet that has just been robbed of all its gold coins**

FIRST PLACE

"Inheritance"
by Carrol Fix
Author site: **mishkabook.com**

SECOND PLACE

"Best Laid Plans"
by Betsy A. Riley
Author site: **BetsyARiley.com**

THIRD PLACE

"Testament"
by Dan Marvin
Author site: **DanMarvin.wordpress.com**

Carrol Fix is a short-story writer and novelist, whose science fiction work includes the novel *Mishka: Book One of the Quadrate Mind*. She is currently writing the second book in the Quadrate Mind series, while working on a young-adult fantasy novel, *Worlds Apart*. Her flash fiction piece, *"Time of the Phoenix"* appeared in the May, 2013 issue of *Perihelion Online Science Fiction Magazine* and in the 2014 scifi anthology, *The Future is Short: Science Fiction in a Flash*. Her stories can also be found in the science fiction anthology, *VISIONS of Leaving Earth*.

Carrol may be contacted at carrol@lillicatpublishers.com, carrolfix@mishkabook.com, or her book website, **www.mishkabook.com**

First Place

INHERITANCE
by Carrol Fix

This was taking hours.

"So, where are we now?" I asked quietly as I sat down again.

My sister pulled her long blonde braid from between us and draped it over the shoulder of her brown silk dress. She leaned over, lifting dark curls away from my ear, and whispered back, "He finished reading the document he was on when you left and started another."

Nearly 50 people sat in Grandpa Michael's library, while his attorneys read every detail of his enormous estate. Several people had left the room and then returned during the droning proceedings. I waited as long as I could, and then whispered to Cindy that I needed to find the bathroom. The house was huge, much bigger than I expected. Not much had changed by the time I got back.

When I received the letter saying that I needed to be present for the reading of the will, I talked to Mom about it. Cindy and I were surprised to hear that Grandpa included us, when he had cut our mother out completely. They were so much alike—"bull-headed as pigs," Grandpa would have said. I loved them both, but I never wanted to get on their bad sides.

The attorneys switched readers and started listing the estate distribution. A rustle rippled through the room as everyone perked up. I listened carefully, wondering if Cindy or I would get the two gold coins Mom had given him for his birthday, years ago. Mom told me about them, saying they were the last gift she ever gave him. Tears came to her eyes when she said he still kept them in a locked cabinet in his study.

I never heard the coins mentioned, but he did leave Cindy and I each some really big bucks. He was worth billions, so what might have seemed small to him, was enormous to us. We squeezed hands and tried to keep our foolish grins from getting too wide.

"Sandy, did you hear that?" Cindy squeaked. I nodded excitedly, motioning for her to quiet down.

Most of the money and property went to Uncle Anthony, which everyone knew would happen. Aunt Millie got a trust fund that provided a generous monthly income—Grandpa never approved of her choice in men. Various other cousins, nieces and nephews, friends, employees and staff were named individually. By the time it was over, people were hurrying to leave.

I bent over, pulling off my cute little open-toed heels—the ones I bought to go with my new outfit. No more bargain hunting for me! Cindy and I would take Mom on the shopping spree of her life.

"What's wrong?" Cindy looked down as I pulled my flats out of my bag.

"I knew these shoes would be too tight. Glad I brought another pair." I slipped on the flats, wincing as I did, and shoved the others into the bag, just as a loud screech sounded from another room. I recognized Aunt Millie's distinctive cat-like warble.

We followed the loud voices to Grandpa's study. Everyone was staring at the broken glass lying in front of a display case of Grandpa's favorite mementos. Uncle Anthony was trying to calm Aunt Millie.

"Nothing else is missing, Millie—just those two coins. Don't worry about it!" He led her, spluttering and protesting, away from the scene. "I'll take care of it. It was probably an accident— one of the cleaning staff, maybe—and they picked up the coins. They aren't worth much. Not a problem."

Everyone else left and a staff member appeared, carrying a broom and dustpan. Cindy and I walked over to peer down at the mess. Several spots of blood shone brightly on the cream-colored carpet.

Cindy looked at the droplets, gazed thoughtfully at my flats, and then looked me squarely in the eyes. The corner of her mouth twitched as she turned away.

I would tell both of them about it, later. I reached into my bag for a Kleenex—pushing the tissue-wrapped coins deeper into one corner. The shoes were toast—they weren't meant for breaking glass. I could feel more blood on my toe, but I smiled.

Mom would get her inheritance.

Mourning Becomes Electic, photo by Betsy Riley

Betsy A. Riley is a multi-genre author, poet, artist, and the founder of Blue Dragon Press. She is based out of Damascus Maryland, where she lives with the love of her life, Ken, surrounded by trees, flowers, chipmunks, bunnies, and deer. Betsy writes under a number of pen names (depending on genre). She is a frequent speaker at area SFF and Horror cons, and is beginning to branch out into costume design. She has about twenty short stories and twenty poems published in various magazines and anthologies, and is working on two braided urban fantasy novels.

To learn more about her writing, see **BetsyARiley.com**
Her artwork is featured at **BetsyRiley.com**
Her blog, "Just One Thing…" is at **BRWS.com/wordpress**

Second Place

Best Laid Plans
by Betsy A. Riley

Attorney Stu Williams nudged one of the chairs, upset. This whole deal was irregular. Imagine, reading the will in the deceased's home, while the upstairs was still draped with crime scene tape. It had taken all his pull with the police to get the family access to the first floor. A burly sergeant stood at the base of the stairs. Two officers roamed the downstairs.

The family would not be happy with the terms. The three children and four grandchildren had each been given trusts at age 21. The old man thought that was enough, since all but the grandson had squandered the money. The estate would establish a museum. The big shocker would be the disposition of the six antique gold coins that were the stars of

47

Michael's collection. Williams himself had a copy of the photo journal documenting the search for the shipwreck that yielded the rare treasures.

The eldest son entered griping about not being allowed to bring his wife, his accountant, or his lawyer. His two daughters trailed haughtily after him. The younger son drove separately from his daughter and her husband, but they walked in together. There was a brief tussle as the husband was denied entry. Squealing tires marked his departure. Last to arrive was the daughter. She wobbled, clutching the arm of the only grandson. She was doused in perfume that failed to mask the smell of alcohol.

"OK, we're all here," snapped the eldest son, "give us the bottom line—we can read the boilerplate later."

"The bottom line is that the estate is left in trust for a museum, to be converted from this mansion. Mr. Michael specified that each of you had already received your inheritance."

Groans and curses rippled around the table.

"What about the coins?" demanded the younger son.

"Yes, who gets papa's beloved coins?" said the daughter, with a hiccup.

"Mr. Michael recognized the coins have sentimental value, as a memento of his life.

Unfortunately there are seven of you and only six coins. If one of you agrees to accept an alternate memento, the others can each take a coin. Otherwise the coins will remain with the museum. The coins must be selected today or they revert to the museum."

"What is the alternate memento?" said the eldest, shoving his chair back from the table.

"It is ... a tooth ... from his 'second-favorite dentures' ... there are a dozen to pick from."

"Eww, gross," chimed the granddaughters.

"Why don't we leave the coins with the museum?" said the grandson. "It would be a great tribute to Grandpa Michael."

"You would say that," said the oldest son, "you with your snooty degree in antiquities."

Arguments erupted. When his mother began crying, the grandson gave in.

"Fine, I'll take a tooth and the rest of you can break up Grandpa's collection."

"Very well," said Williams, "Follow me, and you can each select your coin."

He crossed to the den, stepping aside so the family members could enter. The floor was covered with broken glass and a few drops of blood. The display case was shattered, with only imprints where the coins had been.

"Don't touch anything," Williams commanded, raising his voice above the outbursts. "The will is ironclad. If and when the coins are recovered, they will revert to the museum. You are all welcome to take a tooth."

The family filed out with their copies of the will. Only the grandson took a tooth.

Williams marveled at the foresight of the old man. He had predicted exactly how each person would react. Tomorrow Williams would deliver a letter to the grandson, naming him curator of the new museum. By the time the renovations were done, the coins would be back from loan to the Smithsonian that Michael had arranged to occur when he died. Williams sucked his sore finger. Damn the old man for insisting that he add drops of blood to set the scene.

Betsy A. Riley

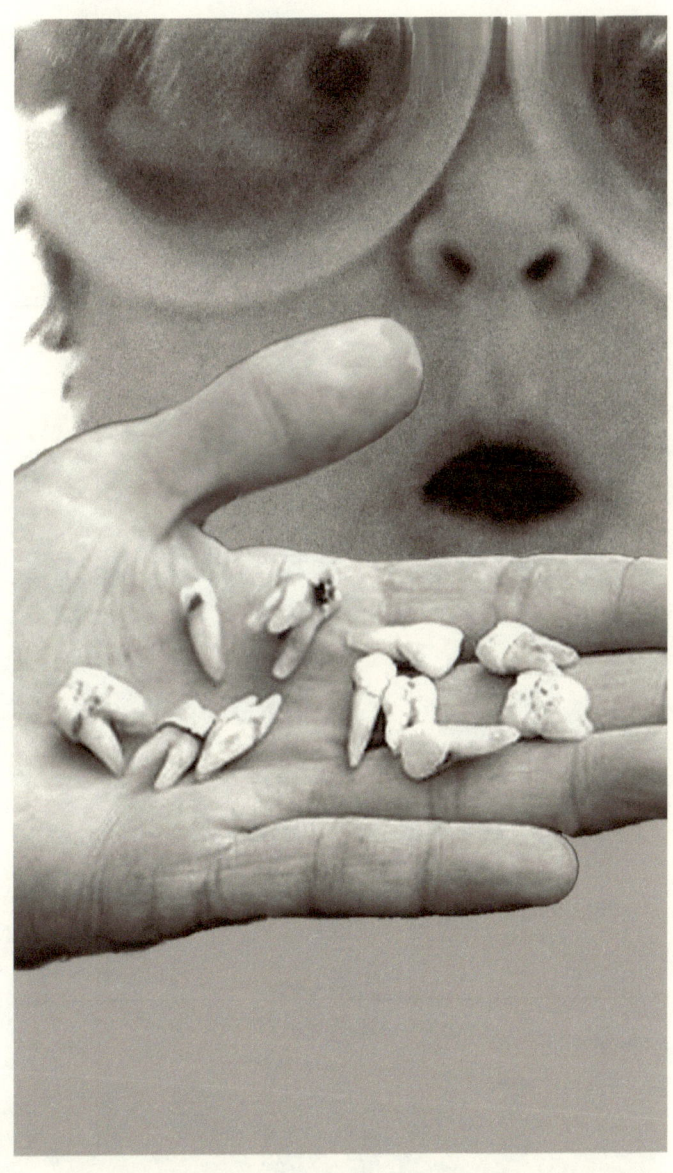

Nothing but the Tooth, collage by Betsy Riley

Dan Marvin is a regular winner of the monthly contests, and we all look forward to his always creative, often humorous takes on the challenges.

DanMarvin.wordpress.com

Third Place

Testament
by Dan Marvin

The wind howled in the eaves of the aging mansion and in the distance thunder rumbled. Leave it to Grandpa Michael to invite us to the reading of his will on such an ominous evening. I loved the man but he was prone to the dramatic even from the grave. I pulled my sweater around my shoulders and entered the sitting room.

My cousin Max was already there with his lawyer, and my mother waved to me from near the mantle. I walked over to her and put my arms around her frail shoulders; the passing of her father was still fresh. She had been the favorite, while my Uncle Cedric (Max's father) had been the black sheep of the family. I could hear his familiar thump on the stairway, he had always been the last to arrive at any family function. This motley assortment was what remained of the once rich and mighty Thereaux family. Uncle Cedric entered the room smelling of alcohol and looking disheveled, which were his primary callings in life. A fresh bandage was wrapped around his hand that I didn't recall seeing earlier in the day when we all arrived.

We stared at one another silently for a few minutes before hearing the front door open. That would be Mr. Grayson, Grandpa Michael's attorney. He bustled into the room with an impatient air and sat down at the writing desk, starting to open his briefcase without greeting any of us. I suppose he was as tired of the Thereaux clan as the rest of the world seemed to be.

"Thank you for coming," he stated perfunctorily as he picked up the document before him. "I, Michael Thereaux, being of sound mind and body do hereby divide and bequeath my worldly possessions in the following manner: my estate will be divided into thirds and left to the three of my relatives who did NOT steal gold coins from the glass cabinet behind you."

He put the document back into his briefcase and we all whirled to see a glass cabinet behind us with a broken door and a small pool of blood in front of it. Immediately the cackle of five angry voices filled the room. I looked at my Uncle Cedric and his bandaged hand, who immediately became red in the face and started shouting defensively about breaking a glass in the kitchen. My mother looked faint and I helped her into a chair while my cousin Max talked loudly to his lawyer and his lawyer started threatening Mr. Grayson with a lawsuit.

Through it all, Mr. Grayson stood at the desk without saying a word. When we had finally vented our fury upon him, he looked at us and said "my client made it clear that three of you will not get paid until the culprit comes forward." That started another round of verbal sparring. I know I hadn't done it, my Uncle was the most likely candidate but it could also have been Max. My mother was a wonderful woman and I loved her dearly but even she could potentially have broken the glass and made off with the gold. One thing I did know, this night was going to be anything but restful. Whomever confessed would not get their share of the inheritance, but if no one confessed, none of us would get anything.

I didn't notice Mr. Grayson gingerly close his briefcase so as not to disturb the fresh stitches on the palm of his hand. Quietly he made his way to the door and bid us good night as the volume continued to escalate.

Ready for April, collage by Betsy Riley

April 2013 Short Story Winners

genre: **open**
theme: **an April Fool's Day joke**
highlight: **a three-legged dog**

FIRST PLACE
"Ralph, the Three-legged Dog"
by William Roy Pipes
Author site: **RoyPipes.com**

SECOND PLACE
"Who's the April Fool"
by Shirley Scurlock
Author site: **www.facebook.com/sscurlock2**

THIRD PLACE
"The Strange Joy of Three-legged Dog Jokes"
by Judy Odenheimer
Author site: **www.sailcetacean.com**

 **Dr. William Roy Pipes** is retired from his career as a College Professor, School Superintendent, and Principal. He is author of four novels: ***Darby; Hanging Dog; Doodlebug, Doodlebug, Your House is on Fire;*** and complete, not yet published, ***True Love.*** He has two short stories and a poem in this anthology.

For more about Roy's writing, see his website **RoyPipes.com** and his blog **RoyPipes.wordpress.com**

First Place

Ralph, the Three Legged Dog
by William Roy Pipes

On April 1, 1946, when I was about ten years of age, my neighbors, Ralph and his wife Joann, took their two children, Sarah and Emily; a neighbor's child, Bobby; and me to town for ice cream. In those days, store-bought ice cream was a real treat. Probably really not as good as homemade ice cream, but we thought it was better.

Ralph was a joker who loved playing jokes on people, but he couldn't take a joke. He didn't subscribe to the adage, 'turnabout is fair play'.

This was April Fool's day, so Ralph was pulling one April Fool's joke after another. He told his daughters, "You have to share your ice cream with Bobby." Now Bobby was about twelve years of age, and somewhat overweight.

59

Emily was only six years of age and Sarah was only four years of age. They realized they might not get much ice cream, and started crying, until Ralph shouted, "April Fool."

At the ice cream parlor, he asked me for ten cents to pay for my ice cream. I was so embarrassed to have to tell him I didn't have a dime. When he saw me blushing, he again shouted, "April Fool." This went on until he had played an April Fool's joke on everyone in the car.

While he was in the ice cream parlor getting our ice creams, his wife Joann said, "Children, let's play an April fool's joke on Ralph. Just go along with me, whatever I say." She then whispered something to Sarah. Everyone agreed, even four year old Sarah was excited and smiling. I wondered what Sarah's mother had said to her.

Ralph came back to the car and with a long forlorn look on his face and said, "I can't believe it, they're out of ice cream." Sara and Emily started crying – for the second time on the trip. Then Ralph laughing shouted, "April Fool."
He then went back into the ice cream store to buy the ice cream. Mine was so delicious it was almost worth putting up with Ralph's April Fool's jokes. Sarah was especially enjoying her ice cream. I thought, does her happiness come

from the ice cream treat or from what her mother had told her earlier?

A neighbor, Max Witt, had a three-legged dog, named Hoppy. Hoppy got his name, yes, you guessed it, from hopping around on three legs. Hoppy was a mongrel, scraggy looking, mangy, sort of on his own even though he lived with Max Witt. Hoppy lost his leg in a fight with a panther. Jerry Clower calls a panther, "a souped-up wildcat." No one saw the fight but it could be heard for miles around. Hoppy lost a leg, but gained his name as a result of the fight.

Finally, we all got our ice creams, ate them, and were soon on our way home. "Let's ride around the neighborhood," Joann said. "Since it's Saturday, we might see some neighbors out, and we'll visit a few minutes. I hear tell Max Witt bought a new 1946 Chevrolet. That's the first new car Chevrolet has produced since the end of World War II."

Sure enough, a shiny new car was parked in Mr. Witt's driveway. No one was outside, but Hoppy was standing in the yard.

Ralph, probably a little jealous said, referring to Hoppy, "Max is looking worse than ever."

Sarah said, in her little child's voice, "I thought his name was Ralph."

We all laughed as Ralph started turning red and was getting madder and madder. Then we altogether, as if we had practiced for hours shouted, "April Fool."

Downward 3-Legged Dog, collage by Betsy Riley

 **Shirley Scurlock** is a "Christian Living" writer residing in Ohio. She writes poetry, articles, song lyrics, devotionals and short stories. She is an independent writer, Christian minister, gospel singer and reviewer. She is also the founder of Agape House/Mission. Agape means divine love. The ministry lives to write, preach, sing and teach the Lord Jesus Christ whose accomplishments are His death, burial, resurrection and continued life as our High Priest and intercessor.

For more about Shirley, see her facebook page.
https://www.facebook.com/sscurlock2

Second Place

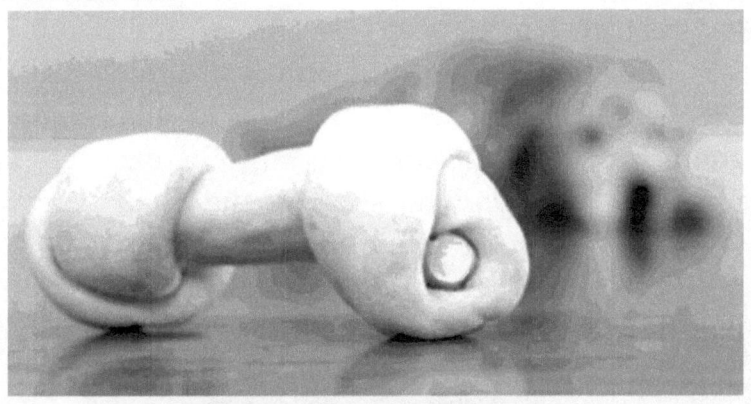

Who's The April Fool
by Shirley Scurlock

Our family loves practical jokes. I will never forget last April Fools' Day. I'm still not sure who the April fool was.

I remember sitting on the porch swing relaxing in the warm sun, when my son Mike ran outside yelling "Mom, mom tomorrow is the first of April."

"I know Mike, tomorrow is also April Fools' Day."

"Cool, Ratchet and I are going to work on something."

John and Mike always expected me to play a certain type of joke. So, I decided to do something completely out of the ordinary. I decided to use Johns' trick against him. Just planning it made me laugh. You know she who laughs last, laughs best.

Mike was so anxious at dinner that evening he scooted to the tip of his chair, gobbled up his food and begged to be excused. I finally gave in and he shot off the chair like a stunt man out of a circus cannon.

After dinner, I heard John hammering in the basement. It drove me nuts. I absolutely hate not knowing what's going on. The noise of the saw running; the smell of burning wood and polyurethane was unbearable. I am a nosy person anyway. How much could I take? Can you imagine a nosy, but dedicated mom perched at the top of the basement steps, fighting the urge to spy on her husband? I was doing just that. My hand was on the door knob; I squeezed it so tight my knuckles turned white.

Finally John decided to get his shower and when he did I slipped down the stairs like a Ninja Warrior. I was amazed; there in the middle of the basement sat the loveliest wooden box I'd ever seen. I raised the beautifully carved lid to see red glistening satin lining the interior. I gently moved my fingertips along the interior walls and found a latch which opened a secret compartment. I decided to put a little something in the box to make it more interesting

Out of nowhere Mike opened the basement door and yelled, "What are you doing down there Mom?"

"Nothing," I shouted. "Get some popcorn and go watch a little TV before bed."

Oh please don't let me get caught, I thought, as I quickly hid my prank in the box.

Finally back in our room, I jumped on the bed with my magazine and glasses, propped up my pillows, and got comfortable. My big moment would've been the very moment John realized who the best joker in this family really was.

John opened the door; leaned over and picked me up. "What are you doing" I asked as he carried me to the living room.

He dimmed the living room lights, allowing the warm glow of two lovely blue candles to highlight the moment. I suddenly felt sick. What if John wasn't playing a joke? What if he was being sweet and loving and I messed it up?

John brought the big wooden box into the room and set it in front of me and said, "Open it sweetie. I hope you like it." My hands shook as I took the beautiful blue bow and card from the lid and slowly opened it. All the time hoping against hope that something would jump out at me.

"Dog bones!" I shouted, "Why would you give me dog bones?" Then Ratchet, Mike's three-legged dog ran toward the box. I guess he could smell the bones. Mike laughed so hard he couldn't breathe!

John shouted, "Mike, get that dog out of here! You ruined your mothers' gift."

In the excitement I tried to retrieve the motion activated laugh box I hid earlier, but it was gone. Apparently Mike had to make room for his dog bones. I thought it was the perfect joke, but Mike still swears he was only hiding the bones from Ratchet.

Doggie Dreams, collage by Betsy Riley

Judy Odenheimer and her husband left the Pacific Northwest for a sailing adventure to Central America and beyond, aboard her sailing vessel Cetacean. On her decision to mix sailing with writing, Judy says: Hervey Garrett Smith (***The Arts of the Sailor***, Dover Ed., 1955, Preface, p. iv) – explains (for me) how both disciplines complement each other: "*… such knowledge as I possess was acquired with difficulty, involving the expenditure of considerable time and effort that was often hard to justify. But in the final analysis, the pleasures that I have derived from the practice of these skills more than compensate for the endeavor.*"

To follow Judy's adventures, see **www.sailcetacean.com**

Third Place

The Strange Joy of Three-legged Dog Jokes
by Judy Odenheimer

The Joke's On YOU! Stand-Up Comedy Club's smoky lounge was filled to capacity with college jocks, singles seeking one-nighters, anxious couples on blind dates and a rowdy trucking company ensemble. Everyone had his or her own agenda. But, the audience members had all chosen to be at this comedy club on April Fools' Day.

The house band's drummer pummeled the skins and struck the cymbals to introduce the MC.

"Ladies and gentlemen!" said George, the MC, smiling grimly into his microphone. "Although today is ICONIC for the comedy business -- you know, April First -- we're keeping to our club's traditional scheduling.

Tonight is JOY!'s regular first-of-the-month Open Mic Night - the freshest humor you'll hear anywhere!"

"Hey bozo!" One of the truckers yelled, rising from his seat. "We don't give a blankety-blank about your 'traditional schedule.' Today's April Fools' and we want FOOLISHNESS. You're saying we have to put up with ROOKIES? That stinks!"

Other audience members chimed in with jeers and shouts. It was not a pleasant scene at JOY!.

I'm a dead man, George thought, taking in the trucker's six-foot, well-muscled frame.

In an effort to calm the crowd, the house band played The Beatles 'Here Comes The Sun.' George glanced with irritation at the musicians, and drew his pointer finger across his throat. Chastened, the band brought their orchestration to a swift conclusion.

"Folks, folks, folks!" George said, nausea flooding his gut. "View the next few moments as an opportunity to be exposed to new talent. Our featured rook...er...comedienne could be the next Paula Poundstone! Everyone, please welcome Ms. Josephine Jorgenson!"

The spotlight shot crazily around the room and then slammed back to the stage before discovering a stocky, middle-aged, frizzy-haired woman standing behind the microphone. She held a leash attached to a scruffy, breed-indeterminate dog. The dog had three legs.

"Hello everyone. You're probably wondering why I'm here with Elmo. Let me explain..."

Boos and catcalling drowned out Josephine's monologue until the club's guitarist performed a screeching Jimi Hendrix riff. The distracted audience quieted long enough to listen to Josephine, and, simultaneously witness a test-of-wills mini-drama.

"I saw this sign on a door, leading into a garden," said Josephine. "The sign said, 'Beware of Strange Dog.' "

The boorish truck driver ratcheted up his verbal bombardment.

Everyone -- George, the band, the college jocks, the singles seeking one-nighters, the anxious blind-date couples, and the rowdy trucking ensemble – nervously awaited the outcome of Josephine and the trucker's standoff. One of the blind-date women began to weep.

"I find the words 'Beware' and 'Strange,' fascinating, don't YOU?" Josephine said, staring defiantly at the antagonistic trucker. Abashed, he paled and shrank back into his seat, gripping his beer glass.

The audience, noting the trucker's retreat, returned its attention to Josephine's monologue.

"I opened the door and walked inside," she said.

The audience warily drew a breath.

"Elmo was there. 'Ah, he's the STRANGE DOG,' I thought. But, I wasn't afraid. In fact, Elmo seemed to be calling out to me, saying, 'Take me home!' I picked Elmo up and walked out the door! There was a man just outside the garden. He had a camera and was trying to position it to take a precise photo of a daffodil. But, he just couldn't get things set up right."

George rubbed his temple. He looked at Josephine. He looked at Elmo, who had fallen over attempting to scratch himself. The audience was enthralled by the on-stage activities. Elmo jumped back up, and landed adroitly on his three legs. The blind-date couples smiled and warmly clasped hands. The jocks roared "Elmo-Elmo-Elmo!" in unison. The singles and the trucker ensemble members cheered.

The humbled trucker said, "Um ma'am. Then what did you do?"

"With Elmo in my arms, I asked the photographer if he needed a tripod."

There was momentary silence. Then, the room exploded with laughter. Josephine fearlessly continued with her set. It was hilarious, sometimes terrible, sometimes nonsensical, but the audience paid attention, sharing this extraordinary opportunity to be generous.

After Josephine wrapped up her set, the trucker approached the stage and handed her his card. "Ma'am, when you make it to Hollywood, call my company and ask for Mickey. I'll move your stuff for free. You're a class act," he said, patting Elmo.

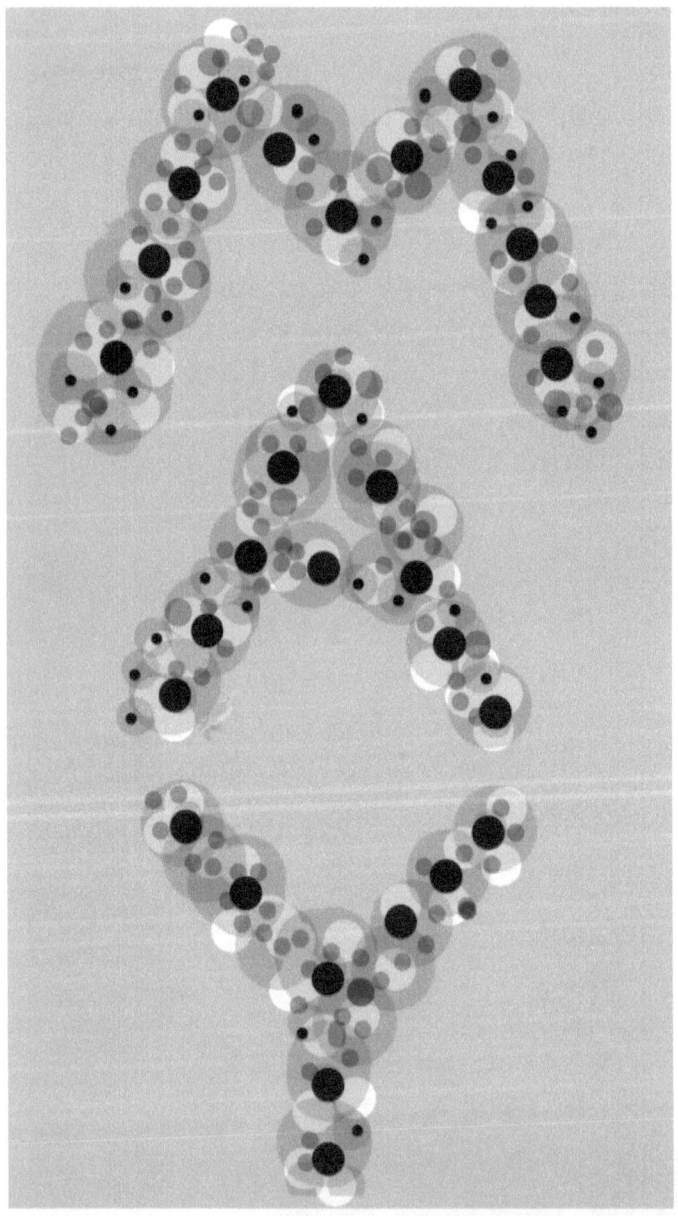

May 2013 Short Story Winners

genre: **fiction-suspense**
theme: **a shocking discovery**
highlight: **a wooden box**

Challenge: *Jake and Betsy bought and refurbished an old farm house. Next spring Jake uncovered a locked wooden box while digging in the garden. When he opened it he was shocked beyond words. What did he find in the box?*

FIRST PLACE
"Soul Plantation"
by Tony Daly

SECOND PLACE
"The Farm"
by William Roy Pipes
Author site: **RoyPipes.com**

THIRD PLACE
"Charming Residents"
by Helen Laycock
Author site: **catchingcottonclouds.wordpress.com**

 **Tony Daly** graduated from SUNY College at Brockport with a MA in Creative Writing and from the University at Buffalo with a BA in English. He currently lives in Maryland with his wife, two children, and their lab mix .

First Place

Soul Plantation
by Tony Daly

Jake Johanson proudly stared at the Civil War era plantation home before him. He and his wife, Betsy, had bought the house, largely at Betsy's urging. One day he hoped to figure out why she wanted it so much. It had been abandoned and Jake had seen it as a money pit. They did pour a lot of money into it, but it was well worth it.

"I've got to hand it to you, Betsy. She turned out beautiful," Jake whispered as his eyes traced the outlines of his home. From the Greek Revival pillars to the grand balcony, he saw his handiwork and remembered every hammer stroke. He had thought of it only as an investment, but after the hard work, he could only think of raising his future children in the home he rebuilt with his own two hands.

Turning around, his smile disappeared. The overgrown jungle on the 15 acres of their backyard was the next task, and it was daunting. Jake grabbed his shovel and machete and headed off into the dense overgrowth. Somewhere in there, he'd find his wife trying to reclaim some of the wild land for a garden.

After hours of hacking at vines and tree limbs, Jake began wondering how his wife had gotten through the vegetation. "This is taking forever," he wheezed at the tree in front of him.

Jake grabbed his water bottle, jabbed his shovel into the ground, and tried to think of another way through. "She must have found a path," he told a squirrel that was looking at him strangely. "I'll have to double back and look." Satisfied his home was safe, the squirrel turned and ran up the tree.

Jake grabbed the shovel and turned to leave himself. But the shovel didn't budge. "What now," he groaned. He gave a harder yank, but his hand popped off and smacked him in the face. The shovel stayed.

"Why you," Jake growled, as he kicked the handle. His back foot slipped and the next second he found himself staring up the tree into the eyes of the squirrel that had returned to see what all the commotion was.

"I'm trying to leave," he told the squirrel. "I guess I'll have to dig it out. Now that's ironic." Of course, he knew the smart thing would be to leave the shovel, but his pride wouldn't let him. So, Jake clawed at the ground around the shovel until he found himself swearing at the giant splinter that lodged itself in his finger. His shovel was stuck in something wooden.

Looking in the hole he whispered, "What are you?" Now more curious than anything, Jake grabbed the shovel and didn't think twice when it slid out with ease.

After an hour of digging, Jake pulled out an old wooden box shaped like a casket. "I wonder what's in you," he said to the box. "Betsy will love to find out, too!" Betsy?! Jake mentally smacked himself. He never had found his wife or her garden. The sun was setting. She was probably was already back at the house. She always hated the night.

Opening the front door, Jake shouted for his wife but didn't get an answer. Not wanting to wait, he ran to the workshop and began working to open the box.

Jake was initially disappointed when he saw the contents of the chest: a piece of paper, a wooden stake, a silver cross, and a bible. The paper was what struck him. When Jake unfolded it, he found himself staring into a perfect drawing of his wife, and underneath the drawing were the words, "Wanted Dead or Alive."

"You weren't supposed to see that, Jake," he heard Betsy's voice whine behind him. "I tried to find it, to keep you safe. We could have been happy … for at least one lifetime."

Jake looked again at the contents of the box and didn't want to believe what his mind was telling him.

"Yes, Jake," Betsy hissed. "They thought I was a vampire too, but I'm so much more."

Those were the last words of which Jake was aware. His soul was expelled and trapped inside the house he had rebuilt with his own two hands, eternally imprisoned inside Betsy's house.

Mystery Box, collage by Betsy Riley

 **Dr. William Roy Pipes** is retired from his career as a College Professor, School Superintendent, and Principal. He is author of four novels: *Darby; Hanging Dog; Doodlebug, Doodlebug, Your House is on Fire;* and complete, not yet published, *True Love.* He has two short stories and a poem in this anthology.

For more about Roy's writing, see his website **RoyPipes.com** and his blog **RoyPipes.wordpress.com**

Second Place

The Farm
by William Roy Pipes

Jake and Betsy Riley bought a thirty acre farm which included a barn, hog pen, and an old farm house. Jake paid for the farm with funds from his 401k, and they used the royalties from Betsy's novel, *The Comet*, to pay for the renovations. While they decided the barn and hog pen had to wait for another royalty check, the farm house was fixed to a tee. They were so proud of their farm house.

"I wouldn't trade our farm house for Donald Trump's mansion in Palm Beach." Betsy said.

"And I wouldn't trade you for Ivana," Jake joked. "However, you could begin calling me 'The Jake.'"

Betsy and Jake teased each other for a while, but anyone listening would have seen how much they loved one another. Working together and sharing the cost was how they were able to acquire this beautiful farm.

Spring arrived and Betsy said, "Jake, let's plant a garden. When I was a child, I used to help my parents plant a garden. We could plant corn, lettuce, onions, tomatoes, potatoes, and okra. If we could get the pig pen repaired, we could have bacon. I love BLT sandwiches."

"Not okra," Jake said. "That stuff is too slimy. How about rhubarb? My grandmother used to make rhubarb pie. It was so good and had a slightly sour and tangy taste. I can taste it already."

"It's agreed," Betsy said. "We'll plant a garden. I can already see and taste our garden vegetables. Jake, have you ever eaten frogmore stew? Some people call it low country boil. It is red potatoes, onions, and corn on the cob cooked together with sausages and shrimp. It is so good. Paula Deen adds seasoning such as bay leaves. I have her recipe. With our fresh garden vegetables, we could invite all the neighbors over, and have one big feast."

"Whoa Betsy!" Jake said laughing. "We haven't even started and you're already making low country boil. The garden needs plowing, and we don't have a plow. I noticed bushes growing in the garden that are big enough to make firewood. We would first have to clear the timber off the garden before we could plow it."

"I'm way ahead of you Jakey boy," Betsy said. "Here is an ad from a neighboring farmer who has agreed to get the garden ready to plant for a mere two hundred dollars. Should I hire him?"

"Gosh, Betsy, You're on the ball," Jake said. "How long have you been planning this garden? We'll need seed and fertilizer."

"Again, I am way ahead of you," Betsy said smiling from ear to ear.

The following morning while it was nice and cool, Jake and Betsy started planting. Jake started digging and immediately dug up a locked wooden box. He shouted for Betsy.

"Come look," he said, shaking the box. "Betsy, what do you think is in it? It sounds like paper sliding back and forth. Do you think it might be money?"

"Money?" Betsy echoed. "Open it Jake, open it!"

"I'll see if I can find a screwdriver to take the hinges off the box," Jake said as he headed toward the barn. "I could just burst it open with a rock, but it's a nice box, in fact, too nice to destroy."

"Wait," Betsy said. "If it is a lot of money let's decide what we're going to do with it. I suggest a cruise."

"I suggest purchasing a bass boat," Jake said as he came back to the garden with a screwdriver. "We're only about three miles from a nice lake."

"We'll decide after we get the box open," Betsy said.

Jake took the hinges off and no one would ever have guessed what was in the box.

It was an autographed copy of the novel, **Web Secrets**, by Ronnie Dauber.

 **Helen Laycock** is a former primary school teacher and English specialist from the UK. She has written eight children's mystery/adventure books for readers of 8+, and put together two contrasting collections of short stories for adults and is working on three more. She has collections of humorous poetry, one each for children and adults and has recently made her first foray into script-writing. Helen regularly enters writing competitions in the UK and has had around thirty wins/shortlistings for both poetry (serious and humorous) and short stories, successes including *Words With Jam,* The Ryedale Book Festival, *Writing Magazine, Writers' News,* **Writers' Forum***, Flash500, Thynks Publications, Erewash Writers* and various online contests. She has four pieces published in the ***One Word Anthology*** by Talkback and several further pieces are due to be published in separate anthologies this year. She has also had several pieces of flash fiction published on the **CafeLit** website with more due to be published soon.

And here are a variety of links:

Amazon UK Author Page: **www.amazon.co.uk/Helen-Laycock/e/B006PGFVL6**

Amazon US Author Page: **www.amazon.com/Helen-Laycock/e/B006PGFVL6**

Facebook Author Page:
https://www.facebook.com/pages/Helen-Laycock-Author/263598357033724

Twitter: **https://twitter.com/helen_laycock**

Third Place

Charming Residents
by Helen Laycock

"I don't know, Jake." Betsy put her hands on her hips and looked out through the open farmhouse door at the expanse of scrub. "Do you really think that by digging a vegetable patch, everything will be alright?"

"Aw, come on, Bets. I've told you before. It's all in your imagination."

Betsy flinched as an icy draught spiraled up her backbone.

"Go on then. I'll bring out a cool drink."

As she stood at the new white butler sink in the large kitchen that had been modernized yet had retained some original features, Betsy watched her husband digging, a cloud of dust engulfing him from his boots to his thighs.

It really was a beautiful house, and, boy, had they worked hard on it, but something wasn't right. Why hadn't Jake felt what she had? The weight at the edge of the bed beside her inert body at night, the dark fog, almost palpable, that lingered on the oak staircase and the chill that constantly funneled into her ears and wrapped itself around her legs like a ligature.

She shook away her thoughts and saw Jake tapping at something with his spade. Curious, she went out to join him.

"A rock?"

"No, it's flat," replied her husband, not taking his eyes off the buried object. He laid down his spade and bent onto one knee. Brushing the surface of loose soil, Jake said, "It's something wooden. I think I can get it out." Using a trowel, he scraped at the edges until it was loose and jiggled the box free.

"It's locked."

"Well, of course it's locked," said Betsy, a little excited. "Someone wouldn't go to the trouble of burying it and leave it unlocked. I wonder where they hid the key..."

There was a crack as Jake applied pressure to the lid. "The thing's rotten. It's been in the ground for years, more than likely." Bit by bit, he snapped off pieces of wood until he was able to shake out whatever it was that had been shifting about inside.

The pair looked down at a rough triangle of stone.

Betsy picked it up. "What is it? Why would someone bury this?" She turned it over and over with a frown and rubbed at it with her index finger. "Wait a minute. There are letters carved into it."

Once she had washed it, Betsy was able to see the inscription more clearly.

"...ell." She looked at Jake, puzzled.

For a few seconds he held her gaze, then rushed over to the dresser and heaved against the side of it as Betsy gasped, afraid for her new china. Panting, he pointed down at the original flagstones.

"I just remembered."

The piece fitted perfectly into the gap at the corner of a broken flag which they had covered with the furniture.

The next Betsy knew, Jake had heaved up the entire flagstone and turned it over.

"Bring a bowl of soapy water over, will you, Bets? And some scrubbing brushes."

As they removed the dirt, the couple could see more and more words emerging tantalizingly on the back of the flagstone.

Jake rocked back on his heels.

"Listen to this: Upon my deathbed, I, Hetty Matthias, proclaim that in my rightful abode my spirit shall forever dwell."

Betsy shuddered. "Eugh. She sounds like some sort of a witch. Maybe previous owners snapped it off to somehow 'break the charm'." Betsy laughed unconvincingly. "Put it back, Jake. The whole thing. It's just silly."

Jake used the palm of his hand to smooth out the earth that had been underneath the stone and stopped, mid-sweep.

"Wait a minute. What's this?" He pried up a tatty sepia photo and blew on it. Betsy leaned in, mesmerized, as Jake cleaned it on his sleeve. It showed a young woman in a long skirt and ruffled blouse and she was wearing a feathered hat.

"It's her. Hetty," said Betsy. "I know it. Can we get a frame and put it up?"

As soon as Hetty was in place on the wall beside the dresser, Betsy had the peculiar feeling of something pulling inside her head and slipping down and out through her feet. For the first time, she felt calm in her new house. Hetty was satisfied, too.

June 2013 Short Story Winners

genre: **fiction-suspense/thriller**
theme: **a subway station**
highlight: **a talking parakeet**

FIRST PLACE
"Last Train"
by David Mills

SECOND PLACE
"Trip of a Lifetime"
by Carolyn Egan

THIRD PLACE
"Taking Flight"
by Helen Laycock
Author site: **catchingcottonclouds.wordpress.com/**

David Mills is the Admissions Assessor at York University in Toronto. He has a BA in English from the University of Western Ontario. Apart from being a would-be writer of many styles and genres - poetry, short stories, SF, non-fiction - he lives in Toronto with his spouse and two wonderful children - 24 and 23 (not their real names). He continue to work on the great Canadian novel and anticipate publication around 2028.

First Place

Last Train
by David Mills

Going down to the subway, I was just in time for the last train of the night. As I arrived, the only other passenger on the platform was a morose, unkempt young man of about twenty-five in a dirty gray T-shirt. His head was sunk low and he appeared depressed, which I found odd given that he was wearing ear buds and presumably listening to music. The most distinctive thing about him though, was that he was carrying a small birdcage with one of those budgies or parakeets inside. Not something you see every day on the subway.

He set the cage down on the bench nearby and ambled over to the edge of the platform carefully looking over the tracks. I tried not to stare although he was making me nervous being so close to the edge.

Then the bird spoke, loud and cavernous in the empty underground. "Awk! Nobody waiting at home."

I nearly jumped. The sullen young man turned around, sighed and lazily took a couple of steps back toward the bench. The information sign overhead said the next train would arrive in four minutes. A woman came down the escalator carrying a large shopping bag and a purse with a shoulder strap. Glancing furtively at both of us, she pulled her purse tighter and quickly strode to the far end of the platform.

I looked at the young man. He wasn't paying any attention to his pet. He was facing the tracks, lost in thought. It occurred to me that, instead of music, he might be listening to something serious – like a lecture or a story, but then he didn't seem to be concentrating on anything either. His eyes had more of a vacant, tired look.

The overhead sign changed to three minutes. Three minutes until the next train. The last train.

I heard voices behind me. An older couple were coming on to the platform. Their voices, though not loud, echoed, but once they saw me they continued in whispers and, like the woman with the shopping bag, headed to the far end.

The gray-shirted young man hadn't moved.

"Awk! It was now or never."

What was now or never? Was the bird repeating something the young man had said earlier? That was what these parakeets did, wasn't it? They imitated what they heard.

The young man took a step toward the edge as the time for the next train changed to two minutes.

"Awk! I might as well jump."
A lump came to my throat. I looked at the others on the platform to see if they'd heard this, but they were too far away.

What had the bird had said earlier? Something about 'nobody home'. 'Nobody waiting at home'. That was it. And 'it was now or never'.

I watched transfixed as the depressed figure took another step toward the tracks. Again I looked at the others but they were oblivious to either of us. They had no clue what he was about to do. The question was, what should I do?

The train was coming in one minute.

I took a step toward him, then stopped. What could I say? Absurdly cry out, "Don't do it!"?

But I couldn't just stand there and do nothing. I wondered if I could distract him. This was the last train. If I somehow got him to miss his opportunity, he wouldn't have another chance. Not tonight, anyway. And things might look better in the morning.

I could feign an interest in the parakeet, that creepy little thing that reminded me of Poe's raven.

The sign above switched to "Now arriving" and I could see the light from the train in the tunnel. I dashed over to the bird cage and opened my mouth to get the young man's attention but I was choked up and nothing came out. He was still at the edge, staring into the tunnel at the oncoming light.

Suddenly he stepped back, came to the bench and picked up the cage, peering at me curiously. Then, turning away, he sang in a soft, barely audible voice, "go ahead and jump".

I fought an urge to laugh hysterically. He wasn't going to kill himself; he was just listening to Van Halen.

Ocean City Macaw, photo by Betsy A. Riley

 **Carolyn V. Egan** has been an instructor of writing and English at multiple colleges and institutions since 2000. Among other academic writing awards, she won the Connecticut College Fiction Prize. She was published in *Newsweek* and *Angels on Earth* magazines and subsequently anthologized in the high school textbook, ***Expository Composition, Discovering Your Voice***. She has a BA in English from Connecticut College and a JD from the University of Connecticut, School of Law.

Second Place

Trip of a Lifetime
by Carolyn Egan

That digital billboard with the talking parakeet squawking about something or other. What was it? Oh yeah. The dream of a lifetime. Where was I? Let me think. I was leaping down, three steps at a time, down to the subway to catch the last train out ... to where? Let me think. I was running out of time. The plumes of ghastly atmosphere, you know what I mean. That rotten cloud of excrement and sweat and who knows what putrid crap that greets you, smothers you really ... as you enter that underground charnel pit with the turnstiles clanging behind you making you feel like you won't ever get out. It's a one-way trip. That's what I smelled or smelled me. That's where I was going.

Anyway that parakeet was squawking in 3-D about a dream of a lifetime. Or a trip of a lifetime. Or was it a lifetime of a trip? That was my life, a real trip. My mother called it heron, like a bird. In her time, anyway, it was a bird that danced over their nodding heads, clawing to get to their brains. But the brains were too low in their skulls, almost in their throats, hiding really.

I think my brain was somewhere else too, lurking. In my knuckles, maybe, because my fists had a mind of their own. They'd bunch up and squeeze into hard little stones and roll around in my pockets and then jump out like rockets and flail and jab when I needed them to, punching whatever was in my way. Yeah, they knew what they were doing and I'd follow them around, hoping they had a plan.

I needed a fix. Ooh. That's it. I was sick with it. Real sick. I was doubled over, feeling like I might have to hurl -- waiting for my train. Where was I going? That cement platform was all shiny with urine and bits from people's pockets stuck to it like little shivering flags. And that squawking parakeet, as big as a person, was over my head, over the heads of all the nodding bums huddled against the splattered walls with their fists deep in their pockets and their eyes shut in tight grimaces, like they were under that parakeet's spell. A trip of lifetime. Get your ticket here.

I was standing there under that giant bird, waiting for my train, the winds of the southbound tunnel sweeping me in like a toilet flush. That's when something about physics that I learned in tenth grade, came back to me. Something about all the atoms of every solid thing being surrounded by space. It occurred to me then, in that minute, that nothing was connected really. Around everything was space. Even in this hole - just space. So that parakeet could fly off the billboard and start clawing at my brain cause there was nothing holding that green bird to the wall.

My fists started leaping and quivering in my pockets, when the brain in them got it. Got that the parakeet was like today's heron, getting ready to rip at brains.

Oh man. I needed a fix bad.

When I turned to face that billboard with that monster ready to fly at me, I saw this lady next to me in green tall shoes, like stilts, a pointy yellow party hat and long red carving nails, She wasn't moving, not a stitch. Staring straight ahead like one of those fashion dolls in store windows.

"Hey," I said, because I needed conversation. "Lady, what's the time?"

Her head turned like it could go all the way around and look backwards. Then it stopped and she looked at me with round eyes. She pursed her mouth like she was going to blow me a kiss.

"Time to feed the parakeet," she squawked as my train swept in, with that infernal scream of metal braking. And my spine was on fire and my head was split open and my trembling fists were jerking in my pockets for cover.

The last thought I had was -- this is a trip of a lifetime.

Subway Skulls, collage by Betsy A. Riley

 **Helen Laycock** is a former primary school teacher and English specialist from the UK. She has written eight children's mystery/adventure books for readers of 8+, and put together two contrasting collections of short stories for adults and is working on three more. She has collections of humorous poetry, one each for children and adults and has recently made her first foray into script-writing. Helen regularly enters writing competitions in the UK and has had around thirty wins/shortlistings for both poetry (serious and humorous) and short stories, successes including *Words With Jam,* The Ryedale Book Festival, *Writing Magazine, Writers' News,* **Writers' Forum***, Flash500, Thynks Publications*, **Erewash Writers** and various online contests. She has four pieces published in the *One Word Anthology* by Talkback and several further pieces are due to be published in separate anthologies this year. She has also had several pieces of flash fiction published on the **CafeLit** website with more due to be published soon.

And here are a variety of links:

Amazon UK Author Page: **www.amazon.co.uk/Helen-Laycock/e/B006PGFVL6**
Amazon US Author Page: **www.amazon.com/Helen-Laycock/e/B006PGFVL6**
Facebook Author Page:
https://www.facebook.com/pages/Helen-Laycock-Author/263598357033724

Twitter: **https://twitter.com/helen_laycock**

Third Place

Taking Flight
by Helen Laycock

Rob dropped his arms as the concertina'd gates growled shut some distance behind him along the tunneled walkway. Despite hurrying, he had missed the last train and the platform had been locked up for the night.

Now what?

Standing alone on the eerie platform, Rob's eyes scanned the environment. Not only was he in the bowels of the earth, way below the bright lights and city bustle, but looking up at the white ceiling, he felt as though he were encased in bone, in the very skeleton of London.

It was as silent as the dead.

At least the lights were on. In front, the track lay like a sleeping serpent, its tail and head disappearing into the dark tunnels to the left and right.

Rob jerked his head towards the black hole to his left. A rustle.

"Hello?" he called.

"Do you like games?" The voice was gravelly. Scottish. Rob took a step towards the sound, then stopped, perturbed.

"Dot to dot's my favorite. Do you know where we play...? On YOU!" The voice quietened. "And I get to make all the dots. Ma always told me not to smoke, but I can't resist that glowing red circle..."

What kind of psycho was hiding in the tunnel? Rob's heart palpitated wildly and his head spun.

"Don't turn round!"

Rob stood stock still.

A manic laugh ensued. "It's dark without eyes... Ever heard the sound of a tongue being ripped out?" The same laugh again. "Keep on crying. Make 'em good and wet. I'm gonna hook 'em out like mozzarella balls. Then eat them."

Rob tasted blood as he bit his lip, desperate for a way out. His eyes darted left to right along the track.

"Don't turn round."

What kind of a madman was hiding there? A tramp?

"Keep still," the voice teased. 'It won't be so bad when I slide these razor blades up your nostrils."

Rob wiped away the tears that spilled out of his eyes and felt his bladder give. This was unreal.

"Do you like games?"

"Please," called Rob, desperately trying not to whimper. "I don't know what you want with me. You don't know me. I haven't seen you, so—"

"Cry Baby Bunting," sang the voice. It echoed through the tunnel, stringy and insidious.

"Listen," Rob tried again. He would have to buy time, get this psycho talking. "Perhaps we can help each other find a way out. What do you—"

"I'm a fair man. I like to give choices," began the voice again, but Rob was not listening. There really was only one thing to do. He hoped to God that the electrified tracks had been disconnected for the night. Taking a deep breath, he ran to the edge and jumped, wincing against the anticipated buzz.

He was alive.

Without looking back towards the voice, he ran in the opposite direction, his feet thumping between the rails, his mouth dry, his heart like flapping wings. He ran into the blackness of the opposite tunnel, hoping that he was not being pursued. The voice continued behind him, fading to a grey muffle.

Finally, there was a light, but not the light he had hoped for.

Rob was found in the early hours by the maintenance crew. No one had even felt the bump the night before.

And blowing along the platform was the front page of the newspaper. The headline, BIRDMAN CAGED was followed by an article:

Psychopathic serial killer, Douglas McFarrow, now referred to as The Birdman, was remanded in custody yesterday after the brutal torture and murder of eighteen victims. McFarrow was found to be living in squalor, his flat covered in bird feces and feathers. An open window suggests that the bird, a parakeet, escaped. Police are keen to trace its whereabouts as it is believed to have been present in the flat where all victims were murdered and, thus, may provide vital evidence about the killings.

Along the track, still in the darkness of the tunnel, Polly squawked from her perch on the duct. 'Do you like games?' she repeated in Douglas's voice. 'Don't turn round.'

July Fireworks

July 2013 Short Story Winners

genre: **comedy**
theme: **Dan's first visit to the big casino**
highlight: **a broken shoelace**

FIRST PLACE
"Taking Notes"
by Helen Laycock
Author site: **catchingcottonclouds.wordpress.com/**

SECOND PLACE
"Playing the Joker"
by Mike Olley
Author site: **hardeggnews.com**

THIRD PLACE
"Lucky Charm"
by Morgen Bailey
Author site: **MorgenBailey.wordpress.com**

 **Helen Laycock** is a former primary school teacher and English specialist from the UK. She has written eight children's mystery/adventure books for readers of 8+, and put together two contrasting collections of short stories for adults and is working on three more.

And here are a variety of links:

Amazon UK Author Page: **www.amazon.co.uk/Helen-Laycock/e/B006PGFVL6**

Amazon US Author Page: **www.amazon.com/Helen-Laycock/e/B006PGFVL6**

Facebook Author Page: **https://www.facebook.com/pages/Helen-Laycock-Author/263598357033724**

Twitter: **https://twitter.com/helen_laycock**

First Place

Taking Notes
by Helen Laycock

It really wasn't that hard for Dan to get into King Solomon's Mines. The saliva he had rubbed into the toes of his boots had brought them up a treat. It wasn't even his spit. Mikey had provided it, and not even consciously. Dan had just stood in the way of the flying debris. It had been rather like having an automatic shoewash at his disposal. And, as he'd waltzed past the blackjack table, a quick flick of the wrist had procured a very snazzy jacket off the back of a chair, just in his size. Of course, he'd put it back on the way out. He'd have to remember not to use the sleeve as a tissue.

The trouble lay with Dan's trousers. They had certainly seen better days. Lounging around in Cardboard City had done little to tax their

117

robustness, but now the lack of fastening was proving something of a problem. Dan was, effectively, more of a one armed bandit than the machines themselves. As he undertook a reconnaissance of the casino, his left hand feigned a relaxed trouser-band pose, while his right arm swung nonchalantly. It did look a little suspicious, it had to be said – not in a sinister way, more as in inviting aspersions to be cast upon his assumed bladder control.

But Dan had a solution.

As the roulette wheel spun, the crowd hardly breathed. Mouths were open, showcasing perfect teeth; eyes were fixed and, underneath the table, was a great array of shiny, laced shoes.

As the ball clattered and bounced, Dan swooped beneath the table. Quick as a flash, he unthreaded the black lace of a nearby shoe and sniffed the leather as a selfish indulgence before scrabbling back out between a stockinged leg and a wooden one, not Long John Silver's, but a stool's.

In the Gents, Dan looped the lace through two belt loops, tied the ends together and tucked the stray tail into the top of his trousers. It would have to do.

Now he was ready to get to work. He had spotted his target earlier. The tiniest sliver of a ten pound note was visible in the feeding slot of a fruit machine. All he had to do was retrieve it and he would be able to get some dinner. He sauntered over and eyed it up. How on earth was he going to be able to grab it? His fingers were stubby and his nails bitten. But then Dan had an idea. If he could just pin it down with the plastic end of the shoelace, then he could drag it free. As he scrabbled down his trousers, he caught a look of disgust from the big woman at the next machine.

In order to get the end into the slot, Dan was forced to come close to the machine. He straddled his legs either side of its corner, rather as though he were engaging in a loving embrace. The big woman's eyes flicked back and forth between Dan and her fruit selection. Leaning in, he managed, after a good deal of fumbling, to insert the lace-end and press it down on the corner of the note, but, instead of retrieving it, the cash feeder whirred and sucked in the lace, the note disappearing behind it. Dan was now spread-eagled against the machine, his arms outstretched in an even more loving clinch.

"Pervert," he heard the woman whisper as she gathered up her things and moved.

Dan was stuck. No matter how he pulled, he could not free himself.

The machine suddenly sprang to life. The lemons and oranges were spinning faster than the stars after a particularly heavy night of whisky-drinking. Dan banged a button.

Ker-ching!

The sound of clinking metal drew a crowd.

"It's the jackpot!" he heard.

"Aw, look, he's hugging the winning machine!"

Dan's life was about to change. On his way out, he handed back the jacket and dropped the shoelace in front of the bemused gambler.

At the exit, Dan leapt up and punched the air and, as they looked on, a collective intake of breath was taken as his buttocks escaped like two white blancmanges.

But Dan had money now, so was off to buy his very own shoelace, maybe even two.

Casino Gang

 **Mike Olley** started life in East London, just a javelin's throw away from what would become the 2012 Olympic Stadium; but sport was not his destiny. Instead, he studied graphics and film at St Martin's School of Art which led him to make award-winning pop videos and animated films in the 80s and 90s.

The millennium prompted a radical change of scene which found Mike living next door to a medieval castle in Spain, where he grew cactuses, practiced carpentry and wrote strange funny stories. He returned to England in 2012 to enjoy the cold reality and more of the color green.

Mike works as a designer in the publishing world, otherwise he writes, having been published in various anthologies and his first collection of short stories entitled Better. He is currently editing his first novel *Harry Moonbeam and the Month of Tuesdays* and still puts the odd word out on his website **Hard Egg News**

See **hardeggnews.com** for more of Mike's work.

Second Place

Playing the Joker
by Mike Olley

With endless rows of slot machines, this place was so vast you could easily get lost. Dan couldn't afford to be found, he was desperate for somewhere to hide. This was his first visit to the big casino and he was in trouble. He was running as fast as he could. Everyone was after him; was this paranoia? Dan didn't know the meaning of the word. He just knew his situation was hopeless and, probably sooner rather than later, he would be caught and made to pay.

In the upper office, Mitch Matteo surveyed the bank of CCTV monitors spying on the punters in his casino. He was looking for a card counter, what he didn't expect to find was the trail of devastation left in the wake of

'Hurricane Dan' -- chaos and confusion were plastered across the screens.

"What the..?" Matteo was so stunned by what he was witnessing that he was rendered incapable of using his beloved expletives. Nothing like this had ever happened before.

Back down on the floor, by the slots, lights flashed as the machines sang electronic ditties, fruit wheels whirring as the human machines, expressions glazed, mechanically pumped in coin after coin. Usually it was good business, except one of the flesh automatons had come unhinged and was shouting.

"He stole my quarters! He just reached in and took 'em."

She was worrying the others. Security had been trying to placate the outraged woman but then handed the job over to hospitality as they were needed elsewhere: a fight had broken out over at the Poker table.

The dealer explained: "I'd just dealt a hand when he ran past shouting out the cards each player held. There was a lot of money riding on this game. And a lot of bluffing. Tensions were high. Punches were thrown. It's lucky guns are banned."

Security muscled in to contain the disturbance. Resources were stretched, then the hiss of a walkie-talkie announced the roulette table was in a spin.

When Head of Security arrived he found one of their waitresses sitting on the floor, soaked with whisky, a cleavage full of ice.

"He came out of nowhere. I didn't see him," she said and fainted. Meanwhile, the roulette table itself resembled haggling time at a souk as people argued with the croupier over a table littered with chips.

"This gentleman refuses to honor his bets," Security was told.

"My bets?! That was my retirement fund. I had a great stack of chips sitting out of the game when the little punk took a swipe at them and spread-bet my nest egg across the table and half of the floor. I bet nothing in this game and ... get your hands off my money!" The gentleman screamed at the rest of the crowd who were frantically helping themselves to the free chips scattered on the carpet.

Head of Security sweated; if he didn't bring this whole situation quickly under control he'd be put out to 'retirement' somewhere in the Nevada desert. The casino was in meltdown, all around was madness and destruction, everywhere except the blackjack area where calm prevailed - he'd found the eye of the storm. A short instruction into the walkie-talkie sent his men spidering through the hordes of gamblers. As security converged and surrounded the table, a spotty college kid suddenly stood up, looking nervous as hell. He went to take a step and fell flat on his face: his shoelaces had been tied together. The impact caused hidden communication gizmos to slip out of his pockets - the card counter but not their main source of terror. The other players stood up to help the fallen student but also found their laces tied and fell like dominoes.

Recognizing instantly what had occurred, a woman barged through the onlookers, striding up to the table where she bent down and looked underneath.

"Daniel! Come out from there this instant."

A six-year-old boy emerged between the table legs, looking sheepish and guilty.

"Don't you dare run away from us again, your father's going crazy outside," she said, grabbing her son's hand and leading him away through the carnage without apology. Hurricane Dan had ended.

Money, money, money

Morgen Bailey ("Morgen with an E") is a prolific blogger, podcaster, editor / critic, Based in Northhamptonshire, England, she is Chair of NWG (which runs the annual H. E. Bates Short Story Competition), Head Judge for the NLG Flash Fiction Competition and creative writing tutor for her local council. She is also a freelance author of numerous 'dark and light' short stories, novels, articles, and very occasional dabbler of poetry. Like her, her blog is consumed by all things literary.

She recently created five online writing groups and an interview-only blog. Her debut novel is the chick lit eBook **The Serial Dater's Shopping List** and she has six others (mostly crime) in the works. She has several short story collections and writer's block workbooks available on Amazon.com, Amazon.co.uk and Smashwords.

For more about Morgen see the links:

Blog: **MorgenBailey.wordpress.com**

Twitter**: twitter.com/morgenwriteruk**

Facebook: **facebook.com/morgenwriteruk**

Amazon US & UK links:

www.amazon.com/Morgen-Bailey/e/B007SNIBF8

www.amazon.co.uk/Morgen-Bailey/e/B007SNIBF8

Smashwords:

www.smashwords.com/profile/view/morgenbailey

[roulette photo courtesy www.abbiati.it]

Third Place

Lucky Charm
by Morgen Bailey

"Can I sit here?" Dan pointed to an empty chair while looking at the roulette croupier's badge, 'Earl'.

Earl paid him no attention, too involved in the game already underway. Someone to Dan's right shushed him.

Dan said, "Sorry," to no one in particular.

A female voice to his left said, "Don't mind him, he takes it all too seriously."

'He' shushed again.

Dan sat and studied the woman for a moment. She looked a little older than him, nudging forty he guessed, with auburn hair, natural, not bottle-fed.

"He does it whether you say anything or not," she continued, her southern accent not out

129

of place in the vast Las Vegas casino. "You can't even take a sip of your drink ...," she pointed to her empty tumbler, " ... without his permission. No one takes any notice of him, but he knows what he's doing – wins more often than not, so we stay, bet on his numbers most of the time, us regulars. Not that he likes that of course."

She smiled, revealing a small ruby set into one of her teeth. Dan, assuming it to be real, thought it one way of showing her success.

"First time here?" she asked, as she picked up her glass then put it down again.

"Can I get you a drink... er...?" Dan asked.

"Vivienne. Very kind. I'll have a bourbon."

Dan looked at the bar.

"It's OK," Vivienne said. "You just need to attract one of the staff." She clicked her fingers at a passing young drinks waiter. "I'll have a bourbon and my friend here ..."

"Dan. Just a Coke."

Vivienne laughed. "First time, and he's driving." Dan shrugged as the man nodded and went off to the bar.

Vivienne sat back down and looked at Dan. "You picked a good place to lose your virginity."

Dan blushed.

"I'm sorry," she said, then looked down at his stack of black and white $100 chips. "You certainly mean business."

He looked at her three different-colored stacks, and calculated their values: $355. One $100, five green and white $50s, and a red and white $5. He then spotted a small bottle set to one side of the chips. It reminded him of a sample bottle he'd given to his doctor some months before, after a particularly dodgy one-night stand. Instead of liquid, this bottle contained what looked like a black worm. A distinctly dead one.

"It's my lucky charm," she said, following his gaze. "Belonged to my late husband." She made the sign of the cross over her ample chest.

"What...?"

"His baseball shoelaces. He was a pro. I know it's silly, but I can't carry the shoes around now can I?"

"I guess not."

Earl cleared his throat and looked at Dan.

"Sorry," Dan said, leaning forward to grab a chip but knocking the pile onto the green cloth. "Sorry," he repeated, picking them up and placing them back into the curved slot.

"No problem," Vivienne said. "Time is money here, so you can't sit for long or someone will be ready to take your place." She looked at the small crowd of people gathering around them.

"Place your bets please!" Earl called in a monotone voice betraying its countless repetition.

Dan watched all but one of the other players put down their chips, mostly $25s on black number 1, then lay one of his $100 chips on red 14. Vivienne did the same. The area went quiet as the ball spun, one of the other men's head moving in a circular motion as the wheel slowed.

Vivienne cheered as the ball settled into red 14. The man to Dan's right grunted then shushed. The next few games went a similar fashion, with the man losing badly, but Dan and Vivienne running out of room in their curved slots for all their chips.

Dan looked at his watch then turned to Vivienne. "I should be going."

She slumped her shoulders. "What a shame. I was just starting to have fun. I don't need these shoelaces, I just need you. It's more than beginner's luck, sweetheart."

Dan nodded. "It's true, this is my first time here but I didn't say I hadn't played before." He grinned, revealing a dazzling smile, interrupted only by a single gold tooth.

August 2013 Short Story Winners

genre: **fiction-adventure for children aged 4-7**
theme: **you are an ant at a picnic**
highlight: **quest for food**

FIRST PLACE
"Minibeast Feast"
by Helen Laycock
Author site: **catchingcottonclouds.wordpress.com/**

SECOND PLACE
"The Wizards Picnic"
by Alli Vaughan

THIRD PLACE
"The Forage"
by Mohammed B

Helen Laycock is a former primary school teacher and English specialist from the UK. As well as having written eight children's mystery/adventure books for readers of 8+, she has put together two contrasting collections of short stories for adults and is working on three more. She has collections of humorous poetry, one each for children and adults and has recently made her first foray into script-writing.

Amazon UK Author Page: **www.amazon.co.uk/Helen-Laycock/e/B006PGFVL6**

Amazon US Author Page: **www.amazon.com/Helen-Laycock/e/B006PGFVL6**

Facebook Author Page:
https://www.facebook.com/pages/Helen-Laycock-Author/263598357033724

Twitter: **https://twitter.com/helen_laycock**

First Place

Minibeast Feast
by Helen Laycock

"Is it nearly lunchtime? Is it nearly munchtime?"

"Soon," said Mama. "Just be patient. Nearly there."

My six little legs scurried behind speedy Mama as she wove through the enormous blades of grass which waved like green paper swords. Little grains of earth shifted beneath our feet like brown sugar.

Sugar...

I loved it. Mama said it was good for us, full of energy and we were saving the humans lots of money that the dentist would take if we ate theirs. I'm not sure that's entirely true. I once met a beautiful tooth fairy called Lilibelle who told me she swapped fallen out teeth for money.

"I'm not really grumbling, but this antlette's tummy's rumbling," I sang out to Mama who had suddenly stopped.

Was that the sea?

The grass had gone. In its place was a beautiful patch of color: squares of red, yellow, purple and green — all the colors of Mrs. McKinnon's garden where our anthill home was hidden under a patch of petunias.

"Come on," said Mama, her head shining like a tiny toffee apple, "This is what the humans call 'a picnic'."

"A nicpic?" I repeated. "What's a nicpic?"

"Why, it's a feast laid out just for us. Stay close to Mama. There's lots to explore and lots to—" Mama gave her antennae a quick swipe. "—taste."

My antennae went berserk and I really didn't know which way to turn, so I ran as fast as I could from shape to shape. If I had had ink on my feet, I would have scribbled a very messy pattern on the soft ground covering Mama called a 'picnic rug'.

I scaled the side of a bowl. (I'm very good at climbing.) Inside, was a huge pile of strawberries like giant, red boulders. I clambered all over them, nibbling the delicious sweetness, but quickly hurried away again when I heard a familiar buzz nearby. It was Wozza, the wasp who lives in our apple tree.

'See ya! Wouldn't wanna 'bee' ya!' It was Wozza's favorite line.

I crawled onto a plate of crisps. Salt and vinegar. My favorite. Like little umbrellas, they gave me shade as I disappeared underneath the layers.

Boy, was I thirsty.

Luckily, I spotted an enormous glass jug. I can spot orange juice a mile off. I would have licked my lips if I'd had any. Mama had warned me about liquid. I had tasted a few spills before in Mrs. McKinnon's kitchen – lemonade, cola, coffee... eugh, though the sugar that she'd spilled on the countertop was lovely.

Mmm ... sugar.

I raced up the side of the jug and onto the lip from where I looked over into the glorious orange pool. I could barely contain my excitement as I headed towards it. The inside of the jug didn't quite have ... enough ... grip ...

And, before I knew it, SPLOSH! I was in.

"Mama! Mama!" I called as I kicked my little legs and tried to swim. Mama didn't come. Suddenly, I hit some sort of iceberg. It was cold and slippery and it was bobbing about on the top of the juice. I managed to attach my jaws and scramble on.

As I sat there, I began to feel very, very cold. I lifted up three legs at a time and waved them about to get warm. I began to feel a little seasick, but then I realized that my iceberg and I were on the move. At speed. In one great rush, I had surfed out and had landed on the rug. My iceberg had shrunk to a small, smooth blob.

"Tommy! Careful!" I heard a voice cry.

To my left was a blue shoe. It was wet with juice.

"Oops," said the voice belonging to the shoe.

As a cloth came down, throwing a huge shadow across me, Mama rushed past, shouting, "Run!"

I did, right over a fairy cake with sparkly pink icing and a jellied sweet on top. I tried to drag it with me, but it was too big, so I took a great big bite instead.

Ah, sugar ...

Then I scurried behind Mama, unable to sing another word as my mouth was so full. And I still had to clean off all that orange juice when we got home.

Helen Laycock

 **Alli Vaughan** is a marketing director living in Portland, Oregon. In her free time she enjoys painting, creative writing, and jogging. Her favorite genre of books is fantasy, but she also loves a good science fiction story as well. Her writing tends to involve the mystical and the paranormal.

Second Place

The Wizard's Picnic
by Alli Vaughan

Two little ants stood outside the anthill ready to go. Goss, the eldest, loved adventures and took his sister Mattie with him on exciting trips around the park where they lived.

Because Mattie and Goss had over three hundred brothers and sisters, their parents wouldn't even know they were missing.

They walked along, their six legs padding along on the moist grass.

"What a beautiful day," Goss said. "I know, let's go to a picnic!"

"What's a picnic?" Mattie asked, her eyes wide with wonder.

"People, human people, lay down a huge blanket and sit in a circle. They bring food, even your favorite ..."

141

"Grapes!" Mattie shouted excitedly. "And strawberries!"

Goss smiled, he had just tempted her with the most delicious foods in the world that could possibly be waiting for them at the picnic. "Yes, and cheese, mountains and mountains of cheese," he replied.

"But, doesn't that belong to the humans? Won't they be mad if we take it?"

"We're so small and they are so large, they wouldn't even notice. One grape alone will feed us for days."

"That's true. But what about getting squashed? I'm only eight days old; I want to live to a ripe old age of sixty days!"

"We just have to sneak, Mattie; they won't even see us. Pretend we're super-secret spies. Now, follow me, like this."

Mattie giggled as she bent her legs and tiptoed along, following her brother's creeping. He put his finger to his mouth to show her how to be quiet as they moved silently toward the center of the park where humans often visited.

Stealthily they moved over branch and under leaf, both wearing serious looks of mystery on their young faces.

Goss stopped and whispered to his sister, "Look, over there! A red checkered blanket, that has to be a picnic blanket."

Mattie nodded. Goss was very smart and knew so much about the world.

"Stay low, move slow, and keep your eyes open!"

Mattie and Goss came upon the picnic and their eyes drank in so much food that they couldn't believe what they saw. An entire chicken sat on a green platter, piles of crackers and cheese cascaded downward from a giant yellow bag. Strawberries that seemed bigger than the sun made their mouths water.

Silently, Goss crept forward. He reached out and grabbed the smallest of strawberries. Using his extreme strength he hauled it up on his back. Mattie came close and steadied the fruit. They moved off of the checkered blanket back into the grass before anyone would spot them.

Suddenly, a large foot came stomping down and blocking their path. Goss dropped the strawberry in surprise.

A large booming voice, a voice so loud it seemed to be from God himself said, "Now what are you two little ants doing with my food?"

Mattie and Goss froze. They had never been spoken to by a human before. Every time humans spoke they sounded like gibberish and squeaks, but this human spoke actual words they understood.

"Well, don't keep me waiting. What are you two doing?"

"Uh, you can speak ant?" Goss asked.

The human snorted and a large eye came close to the earth, his giant beard drug on the grass. "I'm a wizard! Ant language is nothing to a great wizard like me. Why, I can speak dragon! Now why are you stealing my food? Why didn't you just ask if you wanted to make off with my lunch?"

"We're sorry," Mattie replied. "We didn't think you would miss one little piece."

"I don't. But, it's stealing all the same. I'm morally opposed. You must be punished."

"Punished?" Goss gulped.

A giant tree of a wand appeared before them and with a flash, Mattie and Goss were changed. They grew and grew until the world they knew disappeared. They felt dizzy and turned to face the wizard in another form.

Mattie blinked and looked down at her hands, only one pair. And down at feet, just two.

"There," the wizard said with a triumphant smile. "One day as a human should teach the two of you two steal again. Now sit down and have a picnic before I send you on an adventure."

Mohammed B did not provide a photo or bio.

Third Place

The Forage
by Mohammed B

It was a beautiful sunny summer day at the park. Sameera the ant marched at the front of her row, while the ninety-nine others followed neatly behind. Tip-tap tip-tap went their claws against the soil. They were well-trained, showing off their marching skills.

"Look lively! Left right, left right, left right, left!" commanded Sameera. Millipedes, beetles and other creepy-crawlies politely made way.

They all felt proud of themselves. They had just been made foragers and this was their first mission! Their Queen Tasneem sent them to collect food for the babies, or larvae, back at the nest. The food was also for their other brothers and sisters, the Queen, and of course themselves. They were expecting a nice big feast,

147

as they knew in summertime humans came to this park to have picnics!

And how lucky they were to be Queen Tasneem's daughters! They all got to share in that beauty! The same glossy black shell that glistened like diamonds, big pretty black eyes, and six strong legs that carried them wherever they wanted. How blessed were they!

"For Queen Tasneem!" Sameera shouted out proudly.

"For Queen Tasneem!" her sister behind her shouted out just as proudly.

"For Queen Tasneem!" the sister behind her shouted out again.

And so on until all one hundred ants had said it. Then like cheerleaders they screamed. "WOOOO!"

They came to the edge of a big white cloth. Sameera told her sisters to halt, and suddenly the tip-tap stopped. They looked ahead to see all manner of food before them – chocolates! And sandwiches! And fruit salads! And drinks galore! The row stared greedily at the delicious treats! In fact, the twenty at the back got so greedy they started to march, crashing into the other eighty and making them fall down!

"What happened?" Sameera demanded to know.

"Sorry Sameera," said Ajmala, the very last one. "We just wanted it so badly we forgot you told us to halt!"

"Yeah, it looks so good. It smells so good. I bet it would taste so good too!" said Rayan who was right in the middle.

Soon the whole line talked, all wishing Sameera would hurry up and give them the order to march on. Finally she gave in.

"Alright, alright!" said Sameera. "Everyone back in line! Forward march!"

Her sisters could not hide their smiles. Their legs moved fast and strong, tip-tap-tip-tap! Onto the picnic cloth they went. Their eyes were fixed on the lovely food ahead. However, there was a problem: the food was too big to carry back!

"Alright sisters! Get in formation," ordered Sameera. "We're going to carry it off one item at a time."

"No you won't. We're taking it!" said a strange voice.

It belonged to the leader of another row! They had gold shells, which Sameera and her row thought were ugly.

"We found it first. I, Sameera, am taking it for Queen Tasneem!" said Sameera.

Their leader replied, "Wrong. I, Denise, am taking it for Queen Faye!"

The lines prepared for battle, lining up so one black ant was in front of one gold ant and vice versa. They kept an eye out, daring each other to make the first move.

Except Ajmala, she didn't want to fight and neither did the gold ant before her.

"Hmm, I don't really want to fight. I think we can share instead," Ajmala suggested.

"Yeah, I agree," said the ant before her. "I'm Helen."

"Ajmala." Helen and Ajmala walked over to a banana and began to bite it in half!

"What are you doing?" Sameera and Denise asked.

Ajmala and Helen spoke together, "We don't need to fight. There's more than enough for all of us. Come on, help us!"

The others looked at them like they were crazy, and almost laughed! Ants from different nests cooperating? Never! But Sameera and Denise noticed how well those two were getting on, and commanded their lines to help them.

One by one the black and gold ants slowly peeled away to bite a food item in two. Before long both lines were on their way back home – carrying plenty of food on their backs!

"Good job Ajmala," Sameera said. "You saved us a fight and got the food! I'll tell the Queen how smart you were."

September 2013 Short Story Winners

genre: **fiction-suspense (not thriller or horror)**
theme: **a football game**
highlight: **the scoreboard and a ransom note**

FIRST PLACE
"An Unlevel Playing Field"
by Mike Olley
Author site: **hardeggnews.com**

SECOND PLACE
"Victory or Death?"
by Randall Lemon

No third place award this month.

Mike Olley started life in East London, just a javelin's throw away from what would become the 2012 Olympic Stadium; but sport was not his destiny. Instead, he studied graphics and film at St Martin's School of Art which led him to make award-winning pop videos and animated films in the 80s and 90s.

The millennium prompted a radical change of scene which found Mike living next door to a medieval castle in Spain, where he grew cactuses, practiced carpentry and wrote strange funny stories. He returned to England in 2012 to enjoy the cold reality and more of the color green.

Mike works as a designer in the publishing world, otherwise he writes, having been published in various anthologies and his first collection of short stories entitled Better. He is currently editing his first novel *Harry Moonbeam and the Month of Tuesdays* and still puts the odd word out on his website *Hard Egg News*

hardeggnews.com

First Place

An Unlevel Playing Field
by Mike Olley

The stadium roared. Not one seat empty. It was a big game and expectations were high. Seb Manning looked up at the scoreboard desperately trying to tune out all extraneous noise, focusing only on the numbers that mattered to him - the remaining thirty-one seconds. That's all he had to deliver the ball: thirty-one seconds. This was real.

He was breathing hard. His back was already soaked in sweat from running about like a lunatic; his leg muscles burned from the exertion. And it wasn't over yet. There was one last mountain to climb. He saw his son sat in the stand, watching Seb's every move with dread and fear.

Although surrounded by thousands of fans, Seb had never felt more isolated. No one could help him; this was his task alone. A bead of sweat ran down his forehead, caught at his eyebrow, where it rested for the briefest of moments before dripping past the corner of his eye. He ignored it. He was watching the field. He had a clear corridor across but he knew as soon as he moved with the ball, all eyes would be on him. He'd be a moving target. They would want to take him down.

Seb tried to visualize positively but the further he got down the open route, the narrower it would be, with bodies closing in on him: arms outstretched, trying to grab; feet ready to trip; a shoulder charge to send him tumbling. They'd get close. Close enough to spit insults at him: insults designed to belittle him, knock him off guard. He was ruining their game, their victory. They would want his blood. A quick body-feint here and there would see him swerve round one, maybe two tackles. The question was: how long would his luck hold out? He had to deliver the ball.

Sixty yards: a lot of ground to cover. He wasn't eighteen any more. Even if it had been only a few years earlier he would have felt more confident. Seb knew he wasn't as fit as he should have been and with all this pressure riding on him, he started to regret not keeping up his gym regime, instead going for the easy, lazy life: those few extra beers, the fried food ... . A hot dog smell wafted across, normally it would make his mouth water but today it made him feel sick. He had to forget his own anxiety. Today was not about him, only what he had to do: deliver the ball.

It seemed nigh on impossible.

The only way to achieve the impossible was through hope, that indefinable quality that kept the human race going. He had to believe: this was not about superstitions or rituals but self-belief. He wasn't going to give up now.

The crowd buzzed: a mayhem of cheers and boos, punctuated by whistles; exchanges of tactical advice based on flights of fantasy and armchair punditry. They knew nothing. He wished they'd shut up. Seb zoned them out.

Concentrate!

He breathed in deeply, ready for the attack. There could only be one outcome, the alternatives ... there were no alternatives.

He glanced back up at the scoreboard: one second had elapsed. He already knew the score. Sixty yards; thirty seconds; deliver the ball; touchdown; release.

He read the ransom note once again: five hundred thousand stitched into a leather football. His son was being held in the stand opposite. The quickest way to him was across the pitch, through the game. In front of thousands of spectators; the TV cameras; journalists; security; the police. His chances were zero but ...

Seb jumped over the barrier onto the pitch and ran. For his son's life.

Time Flies, collage by Betsy Riley

 **Randall Lemon** took a sabbatical from writing and that period of rest lasted almost three decades. Hailing from northwest Indiana just across the line from Chicago, Randall graduated from Purdue University with a Bachelor's degree. While at Purdue he was a winner of the prestigious *Purdue Literary Awards* contest. He then received his Master's degree from the University of Southern California and did some work toward the PhD at the University of Illinois. He taught high school for thirty-four years, has two children and a wife, all of whom he loves dearly.

Now Randall has returned to writing. This time he is concentrating on flash fiction and short stories. Recent publications by Randall include the round-robin novel, ***Gryffon Master: Curse of the Lich King*** and the story, "*A Mouser, a Keg of Rum and a Gunnery Mate*" in the Anthology, ***World of Pirates***.

Randall will have some of his short fiction showcased in some anthologies scheduled to come out in 2014 or 2015 and is currently working on a solo attempt at a fantasy novel.

For more about Randall, see his winning entry from November.

Second Place

Victory or Death?
by Randall Lemon

Coach Benteen peered at the scoreboard. Five minutes left. Benteen's Bisons were two touchdowns ahead of the Rebels. One believed Coach Benteen would enjoy how his Bisons were doing; nothing could be further from the truth.

Coach stared at a sheet of paper. Most fans assumed that Coach was looking at the playbook, but they were mistaken. The paper Benteen held was a ransom demand.

"We have your team mascot; lose this game or Billy the Bison will end up as buffalo patties."

Billy was old and beloved by the students. Coach couldn't stand being responsible for turning the mascot into Billy burgers.

Though he had tried almost everything, the Bisons still led. They were just too good.

He pulled the first string after they scored a touchdown. The second string also scored even though he had called lousy plays. The Rebel defense was terrible.

After the half, he put in the third string, the dregs of his team. His new quarterback wore eyeglasses with lenses as thick as coke bottle bottoms and was so short, he couldn't see over his linemen.

Coach felt guilty. He was sure that Billy had been buffalonapped by gamblers planning on making a fortune betting on the upset. But the way things were going, there might be no upset unless he did something drastic. He called a timeout and brought the quarterback over to talk. At the same time he sent in a "34 reverse fleaflicker" to the rest of the offense. It was totally different from the play he relayed to his quarterback.

"Okay Schmidt, I want you to run a "34 reverse". The team already knows the play so don't even huddle up. Lineup immediately."

Schmidt was caught by surprise when the football he had handed off was suddenly tossed back to him. He was hit so hard, Benteen could hear the boy's teeth rattle. The ball popped loose and a Rebel linebacker scooped it up and ran in for a score. Now only seven points separated Billy from being served with a side of fries.

Three and a half minutes to go. It seemed obvious the Rebels would try an onside kick, so Benteen set up for a standard return with his clumsiest players up front.

The Rebels' kicker bounced the ball off the facemask of a player and recovered it. Three minutes left! The Rebels only had to score and go for two points and Billy would never be a buffalo robe.

Benteen sent in orders for the Buffalo Nickle defense. Coach knew the Rebels didn't have much of a passer and this might make it easier for them to run against his Bisons.

Three plays later and the Rebels had run the ball down to the Bison nine-yard line. The running plays had also eaten up time and Benteen was panicking seeing only sixty seconds left. Then inexplicably the Rebel coach called a timeout, his last one.

Benteen called his team over, "Gentlemen I believe they called this timeout to discuss trick plays. I only want a three man rush. Everybody else fall into pass coverage. I've been watching their quarterback. He's tired. He won't be running."

Both teams returned to the field and amazingly, the Rebels did try to pass the ball.

Luckily their quarterback was so bad; it was overthrown so nobody had a chance to intercept. Forty seconds left; Benteen was becoming frantic. He had always been an animal lover.

He kept in the same defense figuring the opposing coach would see the Bisons were in a pass defense and run the ball. The Rebels lined up and pitched the ball to a back that started around end. No one stood between him and the goal line, yet he stumbled and the football flew from his hands. The ball rolled out of bounds before anyone could recover it.

"Only time for one play." The fate of Billy hung on one snap of the football.

At that moment, lightning lit up the skies and the referees stopped the game for the safety of the players. As long as the referees deemed it unsafe, play would be delayed and Billy would live. As the teams moved into the locker rooms, Coach Benteen moved to the phone, his decision made.

October 2013 Short Story Winners

genre: **fiction-suspense**
theme: **Thanksgiving Dinner**
highlight: **a missing dinner guest**

<u>**FIRST PLACE**</u>
"Mix Thanksgiving with LinkedIn and Anything Can Happen"
by *Judy Odenheimer*
Author site: **www.sailcetacean.com**

No other places were awarded this month.

Judy Odenheimer and her husband left the Pacific Northwest for a sailing adventure to Central America and beyond, aboard her sailing vessel Cetacean. On her decision to mix sailing with writing, Judy says: Hervey Garrett Smith (***The Arts of the Sailor***, Dover Ed., 1955, Preface, p. iv) – explains (for me) how both disciplines complement each other: *"… such knowledge as I possess was acquired with difficulty, involving the expenditure of considerable time and effort that was often hard to justify. But in the final analysis, the pleasures that I have derived from the practice of these skills more than compensate for the endeavor."*

To follow Judy's adventures, see **www.sailcetacean.com**

First Place

Mix Thanksgiving with LinkedIn
and Anything Can Happen
by Judy Odenheimer

This year, HE'LL be there. I know this because I invited HIM and HE accepted.

Yes Mom, I'm bringing a date to your Thanksgiving dinner.

Mom's yearly Thanksgiving production will feature the usual suspects and theatrics. My superbly accessorized sister Julie will alternately gaze doe-eyed at her spectacular husband Tom; lovingly at her perfect little daughter Chloe. Mom will deliver her annual dissertation concerning my inability to snag a boyfriend. Dear, blind, Uncle Louie will regale us with how-many-seeing-eye-dogs-does-it-take-to-put-in-a-light-bulb jokes. The Stratfords, Mom's creepy neighbors, will bring a terrifying side dish guaranteed to keep me on Pepto Bismol until Christmas.

HIS name is Hieronymus Bosch. I met him on a LinkedIn special interest group called "UTubaWeTuba." Turns out, he likes to play classic folk tunes (my special interest) on the tuba. That is, he plays that genre when he isn't riffing on heavy metal pieces.

Hieronymus' LinkedIn photo was, for me, love at first sight. I recently learned that among his other qualities, interests and fashion choices, he lived just two hours away from my mother's house. After I invited him, he wrote he hadn't been to a Thanksgiving dinner in years and was "pumped to break bread with some 'real folks'."

When Hieronymus joins the Thanksgiving event next Thursday, he'll be arriving on his snarling Harley Davidson. Striding up my mother's genteel, boxwood-lined walkway to her front door, his leather boots will leave nasty asphalt spots on the scrubbed cement. My uncle will gasp while shaking Hieronymus' powerful hand and listen, astonished, to the introduction: "Hey man, I'm your niece's new squeeze. Nice to meet yuh."

Stooping a bit to pass under the door's newly painted doorframe, his spiked haircut will brush the pristine surface and leave behind a streak of motor grease.

Hieronymus will be wearing his favorite sweaty T-shirt silkscreened with the most inappropriate artwork and word selections imaginable.

For anyone having the misfortune to view him from behind, chains hanging out of his pockets will cause his oily jeans to heed gravity and reveal an unappealing fissure. He may intensify the entertainment by bending over to pat Chloe on the head. That bit of gentlemanly physicality will cause Julie to drop the hors d'oeuvres; and, Tom to frantically leap over the couch to scoop up a transfixed Chloe before actual skin-to-skin contact can occur.

Hieronymus writes he has a sense of humor. I value that quality in a man.

When he greets everyone, his smile will cause the celebrants to reconsider eating dinner. Maybe the Stratfords will go home and spare me their entrée.

Mom will be appalled. So will the rest of the family, except for Uncle Louie.

Well, it's time to go. I grab my sweater, get in my car and head, with joyous anticipation, for my mother's house. Hieronymus will certainly inject diversity into my family's predictable little world, I muse to myself.

I pull up in front my mother's house. The scene is just as I described except for one thing - the Harley's not there.

My heart sinks. I stumble up the walkway.

What did I expect from an online romance? Hieronymus had no intention of going anywhere with me. What a joke, inviting someone you've never met face-to-face to Thanksgiving.

"Well," Mom says, letting me inside while scanning the scene behind me. "I see you are arriving as usual ... alone." She commences her annual dissertation.

After boring catch-up discussions, everyone settles in for dinner. Immersed in self-pity, I choose a seat at the farthest end of the dining table. Mom's disappointment, Julie's gazing behavior, Uncle Louie's jokes and the Stratford's scary side dish are all there. But Hieronymus -- he's the missing dinner guest.

"I think I hear a knock at the door," says Uncle Louie.

He heads for the front door before any of us can get up. We hear the door open and then, some genial conversation. Uncle Louie returns with a tall man resembling a thirty-ish Harrison Ford, wearing a sport jacket over a polo shirt, clean jeans that defy gravity and, he's grasping a rose. His smile lights up the dining room.

"Everyone, meet Hi Bosch." says Uncle Louie.

Handing me the rose, 'Hi' winks. I guess I'll settle for that sense of humor.

November 2013 Short Story Winners

genre: **fiction-action/adventure**
theme: **a very windy day**
highlight: **an opened letter found blowing in the wind**

<u>FIRST PLACE</u>

"Hat Trick"
by Randall Lemon

No other places were awarded this month.

Randall Lemon (cont. from September Second Place) At one time Randall was a regular fixture of the role playing community. He was one of the top ranked players from the inception to the end of the RPGA ranking system. He also served as a high ranking tournament judge, marshal and coordinator of various events at Gen Con and other gaming conventions. During that time, he was a frequent contributor to *Polyhedron* magazine perhaps best remembered for the creation of one of the most beloved establishments in the Living City, *"Embrol Sludge's Eatery and Seashell Shoppe."* Along with a co-author he created the adventure known as *"Eye of the Leviathan."* Randall also wrote articles for *Video Review Magazine* and the *Quarterly Journal of Speech.*

First Place

Hat Trick
by Randall Lemon

Jake Shards adjusted the collar of his coat trying to keep the chilly wind and stinging raindrops from finding their way inside. Occupied by his coat, he was unprepared when the wind snatched his fedora. He grabbed for it but the hat eluded his desperate fingers and spun away.

Cursing, Jake increased his pace. His hat zigzagged drunkenly across the street as the wind shifted. The weather discouraged traffic; otherwise either Jake or his hat would have been flattened.

Finally his hat stopped; brim down in a particularly deep puddle.

"Great! If I put it on, it'll be like pouring a pitcher of ice water on myself."

He approached the puddle cautiously assuming that capricious gods would make the hat fly from his outstretched fingers. Instead, as his hand closed on the hat's crown, a piece of wet paper blew over and wrapped itself around the fedora. Unwilling to lose the hat again by extricating it from the page, he just grabbed both of them.

Noticing a store with an overhang a few feet away he made a beeline toward it thinking it would be a good place to drain his hat before he hustled home.

As he pulled the piece of paper from his hat, he realized there was writing on it. Ever the curious one (occupational hazard for a private eye), he perused the paper. Some of it was hard to read as the ink started to run. As best as he could make it out, it read:

Ned: (or maybe it was Red?)

I've had enough of your cheating. I can't live this way. I'm leaving this letter on the desk so you will know it was your fault I took these pills. I'll be dead when you get home after midnight. You probably won't care!

The rain made the signature unreadable.

Jake checked his watch. It was 10:45. The letter was wet, but not completely soaked. It couldn't have been exposed to the storm long. If the letter had been left on a desk in a surrounding apartment building, it must have blown out an open window.

"If this woman has left the light on in her apartment, there is a chance that I might be able to spot it. Most people wouldn't leave their windows open in the middle of a rainstorm."

Jake remembered the directions his fedora had blown. Tucking the letter into his pocket, he strode into the rain. He backtracked from the large puddle first one way and then another always scanning the buildings, looking for an open window.

Finally he spotted one. He counted the floors and made note with his practiced detective's eye of where the apartment was located on that floor. He ran up the stoop and looked at the doorbells until he saw one labeled "superintendent". He punched the button frantically and was rewarded with a grumpy voice demanding what he wanted.

Jake told the manager that one of his tenants was trying to kill herself and told him to open the door.

When Jake got inside he explained quickly about the letter and told the man which floor the apartment was on and approximately where it was. At first, the manager wanted to kick him out. But Jake showed his ID and the letter and explained to the man about the legal ramifications of ignoring a possible suicide in his building.

"I suppose that signature there could be 'Evie.' Jed and Evie Harris live in 4-E. That would be the apartment you indicated."

"Grab your passkey and let's move."

Arriving at the fourth floor, they pounded on the door but heard no response. The manager fumbled with the key until Jake snatched it from his hand.

Jake hurriedly searched the apartment and found a frail, female body. She lay on the bed in a flowered housecoat. Her face was pale, but Jake noticed that her chest still moved. She was alive.

While the manager phoned a doctor, Jake started slapping the girl and forcing her to walk. When the manager returned with the doctor, he made coffee and they started pouring it down Evie's throat.

It had been close, but Jake could see she'd live. Now the only question that remained was how Evie would feel about that.

December 2013 Short Story Winners

genre: **family adventure**
theme/highlight: **cutting down a Christmas tree at a tree farm**

FIRST PLACE
"Firs and Angels"
by Lorraine Reguly
Author site: **wordingwell.com**

No other places were awarded this month.

Lorraine Reguly is both an English teacher and a Canadian-based writer and editor who blogs regularly and with great honesty at Wording Well. Lorraine helps others learn by using her experiences as a model, and offers readers a free ebook, *20 Blog Post Must-Haves* on her website.

For more about her writing, see **wordingwell.com**

First Place

Firs and Angels
by Lorraine Reguly

"Hurry up, Daniel! We're all set to go!" Six-foot Tim Whitaker boomed from the bottom of the stairwell. Upstairs, his teenage son was changing his clothes. Ten-year-old Marc was already dressed in his blue parka and ready to go. Marc held a weighty axe proudly in his hands. He was looking forward to finally being "one of the guys" who participated in bringing home the Christmas tree for Mom.

"Coming, Dad!" Daniel quickly donned a wool-knit sweater and took the stairs two at a time on his way down. When he reached the bottom of the stairs, he nudged Marc's shoulders.

"You all set, big guy?" Daniel asked, smiling.

179

"You bet!" Marc replied enthusiastically.

"Okay, guys, let's go!" Tim opened the door, leading the three Whitaker males down the sidewalk to his red truck. Large, fluffy flakes of snow had been falling since four o-clock and Marc resisted the urge to make a snow angel. Maybe he'd make one later. His entrance into manhood was much more important.

"I'm going to have to take that axe from you, Marc, while we drive to Shep's farm. But you can have it back as soon as we get there," he assured his son. He placed the axe in the back of the truck, then reminded everyone to buckle up.

Twenty minutes later, they arrived at the farmstead. It was nearly dusk, and Shep had already turned on the colored, decorative lights. The fence surrounding the lot of firs blinked brightly.

After Tim put his four-by-four in park, the Whitaker males disembarked and Marc eagerly accepted the axe once again. His heart was pounding. This was it! He'd waited a long time for this day, and now that it was finally here, he was nervous.

Shep noticed his new arrival of customers and walked over to them. "Welcome! Grab an axe and pick any tree you like!" He noticed Marc's hands. "Oh, I see you've brought your own. Are you going to be able to handle that, son?"

Marc looked up at Shep. "I hope so, sir," he replied. "This year I get to cut down our Christmas tree." Pride laced his young voice, causing him to stand a bit taller.

"Yeah, it's tradition in our family," Daniel chimed in. "Marc's reached the magical age to start helping out more with manly work."

Tim Whitaker added, "We always cut down our tree on the eighteenth of December, too. I cut my first one down when I was ten, as did Danny, six years ago." He ruffled Daniel's hair as he spoke.

"Izzat so?" Shep chuckled. "Well then, I guess I'll leave you to it!" He winked at Marc before turning to greet yet another set of customers.

"Okay, guys, do you see one you like?" Tim asked. Daniel remained silent, letting his little brother step up to the plate.

Looking through the falling snow, Marc scanned the trees until he spied a full, lush fir about twenty yards away that caught the snowflakes and held them on its branches in a pattern that was just right. "That one!" he cried.

Grabbing one of Shep's axes, Tim elbowed Daniel who did so, too.

As the three looked at the chosen tree, Daniel demonstrated, "Hold your axe like this, Marc. Then, when you swing, remember to keep hitting the same spot every time."

"Pick a low spot, aim, and swing hard," Tim reminded.

Marc did. The first hit barely made a dent.

"Harder!"

The second, third and fourth ones connected perfectly, as did the next twenty. Exhausted and breathing heavy, Marc finally asked for help.

Tim obliged, swinging his axe and taking turns with Daniel until a triangular shape had been carved into the trunk. "Finish it off, now, Marc."

Marc spent another half-hour swinging the axe with all of his might. Finally he heard, "This is it!" from his dad. The third swing later, the tree disconnected itself and fell with a thud. To Marc, it was the most beautiful sound in the world.

The three hauled the tree to the truck after paying Shep.

"Good work, Marc!" Tim praised his young son.

"Yeah, good job, li'l buddy," added Daniel. Marc beamed. He was definitely making a snow angel later in celebration.

The Poems

Each month during 2013, a poetry challenge was issued. Up to three winners (first, second, third) were chosen, depending on the number and quality of submissions.

January Challenge: fiction about snowfall, children laughing, memories

First: *Snow Day* by Dan Marvin
Second: *Echoes* by Shirley Scurlock
Third: *Lady Winter* by Alli Vaughan

Dan Marvin
DanMarvin.wordpress.com

Shirley Scurlock
www.facebook.com/sscurlock2

Alli Vaughan

Snow Day
by Dan Marvin

Snowflakes flying
No school today!
Mittens and hats
Outside to play

Let's build a fort
Or a snowman tall
Ted, watch out!
Who threw that snowball?

To grab an icicle
On tiptoes you stand
It melts in your mouth
Not in your hand

Red, runny noses
Zippers won't slide
Icy cuffs on pants
Let's head inside

A trail of garments
From front door to kitchen
Hot cocoa with marshmallows
Warms from within

Echoes

by Shirley Scurlock

I remember snowy days
Children laughing as they played
I remember diving in
And the angels snowflakes made.

I remember my cozy bed
With blankets to my chin
I remember trees a sway
With snow dancing on the wind

I remember days gone by
Like echoes in my mind
Visions of a childhood past
Of warmer hearts entwined

I remember Christmas days
With snow up to our knees
I remember sleds and toys
All stuffed beneath the tree

I remember kids outside
All sliding down the hill
I remember freezing nights
Excited screams so loud and shrill

I remember snowy days
Like echoes in my mind
Visions of a childhood past
Somewhere in another time

Lady Winter

by Alli Vaughan

Three eye sets peek from the house of snow
Crafted from winters kiss, her soft glow
Cold noses tuck, lips lick the frosty air
It's white bounty we can all share!

Climb inside; boots pack the snow
Slipping, but not falling, through ice show
Let's hide and give the melting balls air
Splatters and laughter, the fights flair

Gentle it breaks on coated backs
How soft are friendly sibling attacks
Flakes tickle eye-lashed forms
Snow sails, drenches as the days warms

We need cocoa and our energies spent
We'll keep the memories of blessed event
A field of snowman laugh our way
They've also had fun watching today

Snow melts, as winter says goodbye
We wave and giggle, wondering why
And when she'll be by again
So we can build another snow den

February Challenge: fiction about a birthday card

First: *Happy Birthday* by Shirley Scurlock
Second: *Reminiscences on Seeing a Birthday Card* by Padma Narayanaswamy
Third: *Hoarding* by Dan Marvin

Shirley Scurlock
www.facebook.com/sscurlock2

Padma Narayanaswamy:
mandy.com/home.cfm?c=nar040

Dan Marvin
DanMarvin.wordpress.com

Happy Birthday
by Shirley Scurlock

Strange the things remembered
As I hold your Birthday Card
Like in this old blue album
With others bent, and marred

Visions flood my memory
Of the day, that you were born
I was just your grandma
Then, I had to be much more

The times, I watched you sleeping
And the days I watched you play
The fear when you were fevered
The funny things you'd say

Strange the things remembered
Like the color of your hair
Or the baseball shirt I gave you
When we visited the fair

Pity this card's not big enough
There's not room enough to write
The value of every mornings' kiss
Or the tender hugs each night

Reminiscences on Seeing a Birthday Card
by Padma Narayanaswamy

As I was rummaging
My oak drawer,
I found many old papers,
Bills and newspaper cuttings,
Marriage and party invitations,
Amidst I found a card crumpled,
A bit torn on the edges,
Due to constant usage,
And passage of years.
I looked again
Read the words
Of love and happiness,
The words acting as a balm,
To the pain in my heart
For she is no more.
It is five years
She left me,
But I still treasure,
My first birthday card from my beloved,
Twenty five years back,
Given by my beloved,
I straightened the fold,
I kissed the card,
And placed it back,
With love and care
In the old drawer itself.

Hoarding
by Dan Marvin

"Throw them out"
My wife said
They're in a box
Under the bed

Over the years
I've received quite a few
If I want to save them
What's it to you?

Red and blue
Single fold or double
Cheery sayings
They cause no trouble

Happy birthday
Get well soon
Some of them
Even play a tune

Each card I keep
in my treasure trove
Has a common theme
It's from someone I love

March Challenge: a children's fictional poem about an Easter egg hunt. It can be for any age child.

First: *Tradition* by Betsy A. Riley
Second: *The Hunt* by Dan Marvin
Third: *It's Easter Day* by Shirley Scurlock

Betsy A. Riley
BetsyARiley.com

Dan Marvin
DanMarvin.wordpress.com

Shirley Scurlock
www.facebook.com/sscurlock2

Tradition
by Betsy A. Riley

Come Easter in my backyard
what wonders shall I see?
Pink eggs peeking through the grass,
are waiting just for me.

My empty Easter basket,
lined with a neon nest,
will soon be decorated
with the finds I love the best.

Some are simple hen's eggs,
dyed pink and gold and blue,
but some have shells of plastic
that I can split in two.

Inside I might find candy
or even tiny toys--
like a bunny whistle
that makes a lot of noise.

Best of all is knowing
that when I'm fully grown,
I'll get a chance to hide the eggs
for children of my own.

The Hunt

by Dan Marvin

Instinctively they know
It's not just fun
They can barely walk
Today they run

Word comes down
They're off like a shot
Battling gladiators
In the body of a tot

Vividly colored eggs
Play a siren's song
The hunt is on!
Parents chide 'get along'

Wild grabbing
Run here and there
In war and egg hunts
Everything is fair

The battlefield is bare
All booty taken
For clues of contents
Each egg is shaken

Now the victors
With chocolaty lips
Survey their spoils
As each egg splits

Back to the car
With sticky digits
Sugar rush kicks in
Causing fidgets

Everyone's a winner
And it's quite clear
You will return
To the hunt next year

It's Easter Day
by Shirley Scurlock

Though an ant I might be
My eyes work quite well
I see a giant of an egg
In a giant colored shell

Giant eggs everywhere
There's no room to play
In the grass green and tall
It's Easter day

Watch where you hide
Stay far away
Children will come
To hunt all these eggs

Like cattle they'll run
All through this field
They never give up
Till their baskets are filled

Peek up from your home
You can watch them hunt eggs
Watch the fun and the games
It's Easter Day.

Packy-derma, sculptures by Betsy A. Riley

April Challenge: describe your favorite Disney or other cartoon character.

First: *Horton the Elephant* by Betsy A. Riley

Betsy A. Riley
BetsyARiley.com

No other prizes were awarded this month.

Horton the Elephant
by Betsy A. Riley

My favorite Seuss-ite has always been Horton
because Horton's lessons were very important
from hatching an egg to hearing a Who
Horton always knew the right thing to do

I'd always wanted a pachyderm friend
one who'd be loyal till the bitter end
I so loved that he had such gorgeous big ears
they meant he could hear when I whispered my
      fears

Although it put him in a difficult spot
Horton would speak out for those who could not
and his will was not broken, no not even bent
Horton stayed loyal one hundred per cent

He never was scary, with his goofy look
I couldn't decide which was my favorite book:
protecting the nest of that absentee bird
or fighting to be sure the Who screams were
      heard

Horton's brave antics were so fun to see
when he perched on that tiny nest up in a tree
sitting there shaking through rain, sleet & snow
he must have turned blue from his head to his
      toes

And when he protected the Who's speck of dust
he faced boiling oil just to honor their trust
Yes, Horton's my choice for the best of all pets
for, like me, that elephant never forgets

199

May Challenge: poem in any genre about a rainbow

First: *Rainbow Magic* by Betsy A. Riley
Second: *Communion* by Carolyn Egan
Third: *Rainbow, The Cosmic Splendour* by Padma
Narayanaswamy

Betsy A. Riley
BetsyARiley.com

Carolyn V. Egan

Padma Narayanaswarmy
mandy.com/home.cfm?c=nar040

Rainbow Magic
by Betsy A. Riley

Remember your first view? You must!
that sky arc of colors, so rare
a contrast to bricks, tar, and rust
you stop in your tracks, to just stare

In defiance of logic and gravity
its high-hanging misty existence
says there's magic inherent in brevity
and in our memory's persistence

Tradition says wishes come true
when made looking at the bright bow
my jackpot came out of the blue
when I saw a hundred or so

A sea-level pool facing west
aligned with the afternoon sun
prismatic waves rose to the test
spawning rainbows from every one

I've met others like me who've known
alley puddles where black rainbows swirled
light or dark, all our visions have shown
that magic exists in our world

Communion

by Carolyn Egan

The cloudy path I cannot see
from heavy nimbus quality.
Opening narrow and wide,
A pinhole,
various
spectral tide.
Tells me how where I go.
Finds me, joins me,
rainbow.
A dusky sky, a swirling ponderous
heavy atmosphere -
Shining treacherous,
Roiling flagrant
ever where.
Below, between
within, above,
Glimmering, beckoning
hardly seen.
Path of truth, chord of love,
call to dare
of my being
whether near
ever here.

Rainbow, The Cosmic Splendor
by Padma Narayanaswamy

I find the rainbow,
This cosmic splash of colors,
Drawn by Nature
In this earth.
Thrilling my eyes,
Nay my whole senses.
As I find the rainbow
I get excited,
Like a small child.
The sheer beauty
Of the rainbows,
Touch my heart.
From my childhood,
Till my fifty summers,
This cosmic splendor
Has touched my heart.
Found at times
The huge bow
Covers the whole sky
At times just a minuscule,
The Rainbow is a spectacle
To every one of us.

June Challenge: Free Verse style poem (no specified style) about a child and a bouncing ball, with the highlight being a chicken or chick and a barn . (This is a physical bouncing ball and not a metaphor.)

First: *Charley and the Bouncing Ball* by Ruth Ann Hixson
Second: *Bang!* by Jonathan Ytreberg
Third: *My Bouncing Ball* by Jenna Burlock

Ruth Ann Hixson
ruthannhixson.brandyourself.com

Jonathan Ytreberg
outermountain.weebly.com/blog.html
bestwordforward.weebly.com/blog.html

Jenna Burlock
www.jensdesigns.mysite.com

Charley and the Bouncing Ball
by Ruth Ann Hixson

Mom was in the garden picking peas
So Charley thought he could do as he pleased.
He got Mom's exercise ball and gave it a squeeze.
It was soft but firm but that was no fun.
He tried bouncing the bright orange sphere
On the kitchen floor. It bounced back good
So he bounced it along to the door.
Outside he bounced it on the porch floor.
He bounced it down the steps to the walk
Where his sister had written with chalk
The numbers for a hopscotch game.
He bounced the ball on each block but that was
    too tame.
He went to the barn and bounced it against the
    wall.
He caught it each time but soon became bored.
A mama hen with her chicks were scratching for
    bugs.
Charley tossed the ball and hit one of the chicks.
Mama hen retaliated real quick with a frontal
    attack.
Charley didn't even have time to fight back.
He ran to the house where Mom waited to say,
"You'll learn not to mess with a hen and her
    peeps."

Bang!
by Jonathan Ytreberg

The sound echoed
through the empty hollows
of the ancient barn
no longer absorbed by the
giant bales made into castles,
and caves, and places to store
uncountable treasure.

A lone chicken raised her head
to see what disturbed her
slumber and seeing nothing
lightly tucked her head
back under her wing.

Joey crossed the barn
to retrieve the ball,
wandering out into the
world in a vain attempt
to catch his imagination.

My Bouncing Ball
by Jenna Burlock

Papa drove up in his truck
after going for supplies
Mama gathered eggs
from the chicken coop
her prize chicken laid

Papa called me over,
"Come here sweet child,
see what I brung ya!"
He handed me this round thing,
and called it a bouncing ball

I looked up at him, saying
"Thanks Papa, what does it do?"
He replied, "You bounce it."
I begun to bounce it, up and down
over and over, so much fun

Done almost hit momma's chicken,
and knocking the basket of eggs
as she walked out of the barn
"My goodness" she squealed, as
I kept bouncing my new ball!

July Challenge: all about the author, described in using any poetry style, but not in short story format

First: *"I Am"* by Jonathan Ytreberg
Second: *"The Entertainer"* by Dan Marvin
Third (tie): *"I Am What I Am"* by Ruth Ann Hixson
Third (tie): *"Wordsmith or Poet?"* by William Roy Pipes

Jonathan Ytreberg
outermountain.weebly.com/blog.html
bestwordforward.weebly.com/ blog.html

Dan Marvin
DanMarvin.wordpress.com

Ruth Ann Hixson
ruthannhixson.brandyourself.com

William Roy Pipes
RoyPipes.com

I Am
by Jonathan Ytreberg

Just another average guy who
Once lost one most precious.
Not defined by something
Altogether missing but
That remains a part of his
Heart and soul. Everyday an
Angel looking down from afar yet
Near in the little ones that came after.

Yet growing every day
To find some meaning and a
Reason for the loss. For
Every sadness, attempting to
Bring some light to the
Encroaching darkness.
Realizing the gifts I have been sent
Give me all the strength I need.

The Entertainer
by Dan Marvin

I used to be shy
And angry inside
Nothing changed
Whatever I tried

Then I discovered
A surprising thing
Making people laugh
by pretending to sing

I added some writing
Voices and jokes
Suddenly people listened
Whenever I spoke

Being an entertainer
Isn't always the best
But I'm a lot happier
And surely I'm blessed

I Am What I Am
by Ruth Ann Hixson

Short and fat! It was not always so;
I used to be slim a long time ago.
Hair black as midnight, too thick for a comb;
Now thin silvery tresses cover my dome.
Nicknames aplenty: dwarf, shorty, half-pint and
    stump.
What sits on these shoulders is more than a
    bump.
It is filled with plans for stories and rhymes
And novel ideas of romance and crimes
With heroes and villains in situations wild
And gun toting females who aren't meek and
    mild.
I don't like to fight. I'm meek as a lamb.
I don't want to change. I am what I am.

Wordsmith or Poet?
by William Roy Pipes

With writing novels I've had some luck
With poetry though my luck's not much

With words that I try to make rhyme
I'm not so successful most of the time

My writing style will make you smile
My poetry turns your smile to a scowl

My novels usually have a surprise end
About my poetry you say, "Where's he been?"

Bookstores sell my novels for 14.90
For my poetry they say kiss my hinny.

Summer's End, photo by Betsy A. Riley

August Challenge: It's the end of the summer and the kids are going back to school. Write how you feel - be it happy or sad, the preparation, the dilemma or even the excitement.

First: *Ready, Steady, Go!* by Helen Laycock
Second: *Back to School* by Ruth Ann Hixson

Helen Laycock
catchingcottonclouds.wordpress.com/

Ruth Ann Hixson
ruthannhixson.brandyourself.com

No other prizes awarded this month.

Ready, Steady, Go!

by Helen Laycock

'You'll have:

Shiny shoes, white socks,
Jumbo bag, tidy locks.

Sharpened pencils, ruler, glue,
Bookmark, scissors, pen of blue.

Pristine books, a neat first page,
Spelling test and reading age.

Teacher smiling, shy new friends,
Best mates, all, as playtime ends.

Training shoes that stick and squeak,
P.E. lessons twice a week!

Carrot sticks for break time treat,
Lunch of healthy things to eat.

Gloopy paint to stir and mix,
Legends old and science tricks.'

By the end of that first day,
Shoes are scuffed and socks are grey.

Paint on clothes and glue in hair,
Scissors lost, but pen... a spare!

Book is creased, a tear in page,
An ink blot spills at homework stage.

Tired and grumpy, time for bed,
Numbers, letters, filling head.

One day down, how many left?
We both got through; no one bereft!

Keep them clean and keep them keen,
But same old tale from tot to teen.

Back to School

by Ruth Ann Hixson

Summer is waning, the nights getting cool.
It's almost September when the kids go back to
      school.
Returning to school isn't new for the boys.
I look forward to a little relief from their noise
But my dear little daughter is only just startin'
Her very first day in kindergarten;
In the morning she'll ride the bus with her
      brothers.
And I'll pick her up each day at noon.
We'll adjust to all of these changes soon.
Everything's ready--all the backpacks and
      clothes
Plus tablets and notebooks and pencils and
      pens
And all of the other odds and ends.
My emotions are mixed, for the quiet I'm glad.
But they grow up too soon; for that I am sad.

September Challenge: the memories that the colored autumn leaves bring to an old woman who looks at them through her living room window.

First: *Faded Glory* by Tony Daly
Second: *Autumn* by Madeline Coelho
Third: *Autumn Days* by Shirley Scurlock

 **Tony Daly**

 **Madeline Coelho**

 **Shirley Scurlock**
www.facebook.com/sscurlock2

Faded Glory

by Tony Daly

Animated leaves blow across my window pane.
Memories dance with weaving colors, whispering
     your name.
Against the pallid blue September sky, a flaming
     red charges by,
reminding me of your eyes and the fire burning
     down inside.

A yellow, too, a calming hue. It, of course,
     reminds me of you.
Your gentle ways during hectic days always
     shown soothing rays
on furrowed brow, telling me how to smile and
     laugh out loud.
The diving orange is soft and warm, like the
     "nook" between your arms.
That favorite place to rest my head was cozier
     than my bed.
Even greens, the life filled hue, are your smile
     saying, "I do."

As the sun begins to vanish, the horizon flares
     with a dying flourish,
dissolving the colors from my sight, as day
     extinguishes into night.
I still sit, left alone, only with the memories I
     hold
of a love so true and fare that suddenly sunk
     into despair.

On my lap, I hold a flag that lays faded, hollowed
      and grey.
Long ago it sat on an empty grave, but I still
      hold it and I pray
that one of these cool fall days, I'll see you
      through the blown leaf haze
parting the veil flung from trees, and finally
      coming home to me.

Autumn

by Madeline Coelho

She looked outside
the Autumn leaves were falling
past the window of her living room.
Their colors were brilliant -
russet, brown and yellow
bringing with them memories -
memories of her youth
when leaves were young and green
when she was young and beautiful
not old and wizened,
wrinkled and dried out
from porcelain to parchment.
Life was different then.
Closer to the end now
to winter when the leaves would fall
when the trees would be bare
and the ground covered in mulch -
The seasons - the inexorable seasons
always repeating
always repeating

Autumn Days

by Shirley Scurlock

Resting in my easy chair
Just inside my living room
Staring at the seasons change
Dread the winter coming soon
The wind carries trees lost vesture
Spread across Earth's green floor
I watch them through time's mirror
And I'm a child once more
My childhood like a movie
Plays through the clearest glass
Memories dance on autumn leaves
Viewing Nature's photograph
Though my body old and tired
I'm translated to another place
And in memory I hold golden leaves
As a girl on autumn days

Falling Leaves

October Challenge: a star (or many stars) in the sky that twinkles.

First: *The Star* by Madeline Coelho
Second: *Under the Stars* by Ruth Ann Hixson
Third: *Sonnet 64* by Tim Mooney

Madeline Coelho

Ruth Ann Hixson
ruthannhixson.brandyourself.com

Tim Mooney

The Star
by Madeline Coelho

It twinkles in the night sky
On and off
One and many,
the myriad of brilliance-
multi-faceted like diamonds.
Stars light the earth
beneath the sky,
encroaching on the darkness
until the sunrise
sweeps away the cobwebs
summoning us to a new day
before the night sky comes again.

Under the Stars

by Ruth Ann Hixson

Under the stars as I homeward trod
I thought of the marvelous works of God.
I breathed a prayer of thanks and praise
I raised my face to an upward gaze
At the sparkling jewels in the dark sky's dome
To light the way of my journey home.
A passing cloud drew its veil
O'er the twinkling gems that lit my trail.
I shivered as the night breeze shook
The limbs of the trees by the chuckling brook.
My path passed through the dark woods where
The tree limbs seemed intent to scare
Me as I walked along the way alone
Hurrying now so close to home.
Then in the window a light I spied
I could hardly wait to get inside
To a hearth where the wood burned bright
And I was safe at home that night.

Sonnet 64
by Tim Mooney

Reaching up we strive to touch your light
Bending past the moon and out beyond
All your wearied photons thinned and mute
Down here on our lonely, spinning pond
Though you are so far away
We have named you anyway

May, perhaps you touch us while we sleep
Little twinkles in our nodding heads
Bending space and time within our dreams
Burning fiercely in our cozy beds
And though we might never touch
Just to dream, yes, that's enough

November Challenge: raking leaves in the fall, either look back to childhood raking leaves or raking leaves with your own children now - or a combination of both.

First: *Raking the Leaves* by Madeline Coelho
Second: *Gathering Leaves Long Ago* by Linda Dyson
Third: *The Beast Beneath the Leaves* by Tim Mooney

 **Madeline Coelho**

[No photo available for Linda Dyson]

 **Tim Mooney**

Raking the Leaves
by Madeline Coelho

Autumn leaves
russet, brown and red
in a pile
rustling when
I rake them-
not dry,
thankfully,
not dry
as a tinder box -
wet after the rain
coagulating
turning to mulch
returning to the earth
as I shall too
dust to dust...

Gathering Leaves Long Ago
by Linda Dyson

The hard handle
Slid between my under-sized fingers
Leaving them blistered, sensitive and sore
And yet the harlequin blanket of autumn colours
Dancing in the breeze
Hypnotic and enthralling
Numbed my mind to pain in hands
And semi-frozen, chilblained feet
Which I would warm by crunching
The crackling leaves like giant cornflakes
Or kick them in the air to see them fly-
Then hastily return to finish off the task in hand
And push a freshly gathered load
Into the groaning bin and take delight
In pressing down with all my strength
Releasing that delicious, heady scent that
Spoke of chestnuts, bonfires and October
Rolled into one.
And then the weakened sun would soon fall fast
        asleep
Behind the black horizon
And peeling off the mittens, kicking off the boots
I'd settle by the glowing fireside
Where fairy caverns throbbed and danced then
        later died
While crumpet butter trickled down my chin-

All welcoming Autumn in.

The Beast Beneath the Leaves
by Tim Mooney

There beneath the cast-off fall of maple, elm and
  oak
There beneath the outgrown dressings of the
  fairy folk
Lives a beast with sticks for teeth and little
  beady eyes

It will wait so patiently for Dad to finish raking
Till the children run and jump (They're ready for
  the taking)
Children leap into the pile, and what a dire
  surprise!

With a squeal of young delight they bound into
  the stack
Innocently unaware they won't be coming back
With a gobble and a chomp! the children are all
  gone!

Dad, he leans upon the rake, and smiles his
  Daddy smile
Watching as his children ruin his neatly raked
  up pile
Laughing as the little beasts run screaming
  'cross the lawn.

December Challenge: a tray full of cookies.

First : *The Christmas Cookies* by Madeline Coelho

 **Madeline Coelho** is a retired librarian living in the Blue Mountains, NSW, Australia. She lost her husband, John to leukemia more than twelve years ago. Madeline is interested in conservation, animal welfare, advocacy for the disabled and is a writer and award-winning artist. She writes mostly poetry and short stories and has self-published a novella, a memoir called 'Magda's Testimony'.

No other awards this month.

The Christmas Cookies
by Madeline Coelho

Freshly baked from the oven
on the bench the tray lies
delicious aromas arising
of cinnamon and vanilla.
The children sniff
"Sniff but don't touch,"
says the cook,
"These are for the party."
"But surely we can have one, Mama?"
"All right, one for each of you,"
the cook has relented.
Emma and Mitch each take one,
crunch, crunch
they bite
Mmm, they are in Christmas heaven!